# The Best Erotic Short Stories of 2023, Volume 1

*Explicit Adult Erotica Featuring First Times, Threesomes, Rough Sex, Anal Sex, Roleplay, Gangbangs, Lesbian Sex, Cuckold, Older-Young, and More...*

Rayna Russell

# © Copyright Rayna Russell 2023 - All rights reserved.

The content contained within this book may not be reproduced, duplicated or transmitted without direct written permission from the author or the publisher.

Under no circumstances will any blame or legal responsibility be held against the publisher, or author, for any damages, reparation, or monetary loss due to the information contained within this book. Either directly or indirectly. You are responsible for your own choices, actions, and results.

**Legal Notice:**

This book is copyright protected. This book is only for personal use. You cannot amend, distribute, sell, use, quote or paraphrase any part, or the content within this book, without the consent of the author or publisher.

**Disclaimer Notice:**

Please note the information contained within this document is for educational and entertainment purposes only. All effort has been executed to present accurate, up-to-date, and reliable, complete information. No warranties of any kind are declared or implied. Readers acknowledge that the author is not engaging in the rendering of legal, financial, medical or professional advice. The content within this book has been derived from various sources. Please consult a licensed professional before attempting any techniques outlined in this book.

By reading this document, the reader agrees that under no

circumstances is the author responsible for any losses, direct or indirect, which are incurred as a result of the use of the information contained within this document, including, but not limited to, — errors, omissions, or inaccuracies.

# Contents

| | |
|---|---|
| Introduction | 7 |
| 1. Long Time Cumming<br>*By Nia Long* | 9 |
| 2. Dear Diary<br>*Moran Fitzpatrick* | 27 |
| 3. Watermelon<br>*Chrissy Lowell* | 43 |
| 4. Wild Ella<br>*By Clifford Brannum* | 59 |
| 5. Christine's First Gangbang<br>*By Richard Kinney* | 75 |
| 6. The Massage<br>*By Marine Leland* | 91 |
| 7. He Likes To Watch<br>*By Victoria Jimenez* | 107 |
| 8. Mistress<br>*My Amanda Moss* | 121 |
| 9. Who's The Boss<br>*By Jordan W. Miller* | 137 |
| 10. Sorry, Daddy<br>*By Lisa Wilton-James* | 153 |
| Afterword | 169 |

# Introduction

Hello friends!!!

This is your friendly purveyor of smut, Rayna. I'm so glad to be back with another anthology of the best erotic stories of the year. I received so much generous feedback from last year's anthology, and I've integrated a lot of your thoughts into this new volume. Most notably, I sought out some more writers of color to bring some new, sexy perspectives. If you're listening to the audiobook version, I've also brought in some fantastic new voices to bring these short stories to life!

For those of you who are new - welcome! I'm a writer and editor and a voracious reader of erotic fiction.

My favorite format for erotica, by far, is short stories. The writer is challenged to bring a plot to life in a few minutes, which really creates fast, fun plots. And you can sample different kinds of stories without much commitment. You may discover some things you didn't even know turned you on.

This book has everything, from sweet first-time stories to the raunchiest gang bangs. And each writer brings a unique voice. I'm personally absolutely in love with this collection, and I hope you are too.

And feedback is always welcome! Send me a message at RaynaRussellErotica@gmail.com

Are you a writer? Submit a story for consideration in a future volume! I find that 3000 words is the perfect length.

Relax and enjoy The Best Erotic Short Stories of 2023... Volume 1!

XOXO,
    Rayna

# Long Time Cumming
By Nia Long

"How in the world did I get here?" Bria murmured as she shook her head, staring at the wall across from her in disbelief.

Nathan paused, pulling his lips away from her neck, where he'd been leaving a trail of sloppy kisses. He frowned as he leaned back to look at her. "Are you really that drunk? You don't remember us getting locked in here fifteen minutes ago? I guess you really are a lightweight. I only saw you drink like two beers."

"Shut up." Bria scowled. "I'm not that drunk—" Although her head was spinning and her words were slurred and, yeah, she was a lightweight. This was only her second college party, after all, and she'd never drunk at parties before. She'd refused to have a single sip of an alcoholic beverage before she turned 21, unlike most of her friends. "I wasn't asking literally—" How could she possibly forget how they'd ended up here? It had been borderline traumatic!

It had all started when Bria had decided to sit with a group of her best friend's friends, who Bria didn't know well or happen to like all that much. She found them all obnoxious, and she wasn't a fan of anyone who willingly chose to spend their time hanging around Nathan, who she'd known—and hated with every fiber in her being—since kindergarten. And wouldn't you know it, at the very center of the big group of assholes was Nathan, who they all seemed to adore.

Bria had been hesitant to join them the moment she saw Nathan sitting with them, but her options had been limited. It was either stick with her best friend, one of the only people she happened to know at this party, and hang out with the jolly group of assholes, or wander off to make some friends of her own. Naturally, she'd chosen the former option.

But that resulted in her being put on the spot about an hour later when the rowdy group started discussing their sex lives and eventually prying into hers, and her drunken, blabber-mouthed best friend had revealed that Bria had never fucked anyone in her life, which only resulted in everyone that had been around to hear it oohing and ahhing and teasing her until she just wanted to evaporate on the spot.

And Bria got the surprise of a lifetime when Nathan—who had made it his business to tease, insult, and spite her every chance he got since they were still in pull-ups—jumped to her defense.

Long story short, that had only resulted in the group collectively deciding to tease him too, and somehow, the two of them had been hauled off and locked in a closet together soon after. It was all a blur, really, and Bria wasn't even trying to remember it.

The embarrassment was too much for her to bear, and this was definitely going to be added to the list of memories that she kept locked away in a box long-forgotten in the back of her mind.

"Well then, how were you asking?" Nathan slurred, tilting his head.

"What?" Bria blinked.

"If you weren't asking literally, then how were you asking?"

"...Metaphorically? I don't know," Bria sighed, slumping back against the wall and twirling one of her thin braids around her fingers as her doe eyes traveled up toward the ceiling. "I just mean...How did I end up in a closet, at a party, with my worst enemy about to take my virginity? That's...I can't even comprehend how I ended up in this predicament. I mean—I hate you, you know!" She pointed a stern finger at him, and he merely raised his brows.

"Yeah, you've mentioned it." A thousand times, probably. "I'm not your biggest fan either, sweetheart, but even annoying little know-it-all goody-two-shoes who need to be knocked off their high horses like you can be pretty hot sometimes, so I'm not gonna complain about being trapped with you if it means I get to fuck you. Which...It would be nice if we could get to that part anytime soon, by the way. Don't you think we've done enough talking for tonight?"

"You're such a fucking pig," Bria huffed. "And I resent that. I'm not an annoying, know-it-all, goody-two-shoes who needs to be—"

"Yeah, yeah." Nathan waved her off, rolling his eyes as he ran a hand through his ginger hair. "I'm just saying, I can't imagine a sweet little virgin girl like you is gonna be able to rush into anything. We'll probably have to take it slow, so if you want to pop your cherry tonight, we're gonna need to move things along before someone remembers we're in here and comes to get us."

What Nathan said made sense, but Bria still squinted her eyes at him. "Don't say it like that. Just because I haven't fucked half the city like you have doesn't mean—"

"Why do you always have to argue with me?" Nathan grumbled as he massaged his temples.

"Because you're always wrong about everything," Bria stated matter-of-factly.

"Do you always behave like a twelve-year-old child when you get drunk?"

"I'm not behaving like a twelve-year-old child, you are!"

"You're such a fucking brat," Nathan growled. "This is why I can't stand you!"

"You weren't complaining about me being a brat when you offered to fuck me," Bria scoffed.

"Right, because I figured you wouldn't be able to talk much while you were busy hanging off my cock," he snapped.

"That's assuming your dick is any good," Bria muttered. "You talk so much shit and yet you probably don't even know how to fuck a woman the right way. Out of the hundreds of thousands of girls that you've been with, how many have you actually managed to make cum?" She rolled her eyes.

Nathan growled, and Bria gasped as he suddenly

grabbed hold of her legs, yanking on them until she'd slid down the wall and onto her back. He pushed her skirt up until it was bunched up around her waist and began tugging her panties down, biting his lip as he stared at the hot-pink, lace fabric. It contrasted perfectly with her chocolate skin, and there was a dark spot right in the center of them which made Nathan smirk.

"Guess the sweet little virgin girl is pretty turned on by the thought of being fucked by her 'worst enemy' inside the closet at someone's party. How cute."

"Don't give yourself too much credit," Bria grumbled, her cheeks burning as she quickly held a hand out to stop him from pulling her panties down. "I'm just—I've just been..." Really, what was she supposed to say to defend herself here?

If she was going to be honest, she was turned on by the situation at hand. As much as she couldn't stand Nathan, she had to admit that she'd always found him attractive. His pale skin, red hair, and piercing green eyes...His sharp jawline, deep voice, and lean yet muscular body...

The way he tended to look at her as if he wanted to rip her clothes off at any given moment...

She'd told him that she just wanted to lose her

virginity and didn't give a damn who took it, even if it had to be him of all people, and that was true, but also, maybe she wasn't as nonchalant as she'd made herself out to be. If she'd been stuck in here with anyone else, she never would have agreed to let them fuck her. But Nathan was someone that she'd known for a long time and trusted, in some strange way, despite his tendency to behave like a humongous asshole on most occasions. Plus, he looked like a model. So there was that.

"What, are you always this wet?" Nathan raised a brow. "In a permanent state of arousal just like a bitch in heat...I'm not surprised. I always thought you were secretly a slut." He smirked.

"I am not—stop that!" She smacked his hand away when he attempted to tug her panties down again, staring at him with wide eyes as he sent her a questioning look.

"I know this is your first time, but even you have to know that you've got to take your panties off if you want to get fucked."

Bria let out a deep breath, resting the palms of her hands against her cheeks to try to cool them down. "I know it's just—I've never...Well, you already know that," she muttered to herself.

Nathan let out a chuckle that sounded more like

a breath, his gaze softening as he stared at the shy-looking girl. "You know we don't have to do anything if you don't want to. It's fine if you've changed your mind."

"Yeah, right," Bria scoffed. "As if you wouldn't tease me about it for the rest of eternity if I decided to chicken out."

"I wouldn't." Nathan frowned. "Really, there are plenty of other things for me to make fun of you for. It's not like I need any new material anyway. If you don't feel comfortable, we don't need to do anything."

A small smile appeared on Bria's face as she stared at him for a few moments. The longer she looked into his honest eyes, the more she felt her anxiety starting to dissipate.

She made a conscious effort to loosen up, moving her hands away. "Go ahead."

"Are you sure?"

"Shouldn't we be moving things along before someone remembers we're in here and comes to find us?" she taunted, grinning when he rolled his eyes at her.

Nathan carefully pulled Bria's panties down, staring into her eyes the whole time and watching her expression closely. She seemed nervous, but that was to be expected, and at least now that she didn't look afraid.

When he was sure that she was okay with it, he pulled the panties all the way off and tossed them to the side, his eyes trailing down to stare at her cunt as he did. He licked his lips, his cock throbbing in his jeans as he pushed her thighs apart and repositioned himself so that he was lying between her legs.

"What are you—"

"I just wanna loosen you up a bit before I go trying to put my enormous cock inside you," Nathan chuckled. "Just relax and enjoy."

"Okay, well anyone who has to label their own cock as 'enormous' probably does not have an enormous cock, so maybe—" Bria cut herself off with a gasp, shooting up to rest her weight on her elbows as Nathan leaned down, immediately sticking his tongue out to get a taste of her.

He groaned as he pushed his tongue between her folds, flattening it as he licked a long strip up her center and then swirled it around her clit before allowing it to travel back down again.

Bria was already trembling, her thighs squeezing the sides of his head tightly as she stared at him with wide eyes. "Wow, okay—ugh, that feels really good!" she gasped, and Nathan chuckled, enjoying the way she squirmed and jolted every time he wriggled his tongue inside her hole or sucked on the lips of her cunt.

It didn't take long for Bria to start moving, grinding against his tongue and letting out quiet moans as she closed her eyes and focused on the foreign feeling. She pushed her top up, squeezing her breasts and arching her back, her moans growing louder as Nathan wrapped his arms around her thighs to hold her in place as he ate her with more vigor.

He spat on her hole, glancing up at her as he moved a hand down, rubbing his thumb over her clit before allowing it to trail down and push at her entrance.

Bria was too lost in her pleasure to be concerned with the fact that she was about to be penetrated by someone else's fingers for the very first time in her life, which was great. Nathan poked the tip of his thumb inside, then switched fingers, slowly pushing his pointer finger inside of her, then his middle finger and scissoring them to stretch her out.

Bria gasped when Nathan's fingers brushed up against her G-spot briefly before dipping back out of her again, and she could hardly stop twitching as he continued pushing his fingers in and out of her, soon adding a third just as he gave the inside of her thigh a sharp nip that caused her to hiss.

"Getting a bit loud there, aren't you?" he commented, wearing a sly grin, and Bria tried not to show her embarrassment as she realized that he was right. She hadn't even been attempting to hold her moans back, and maybe she should have, considering just how smug Nathan looked now.

"I..." Bria was yet again at a loss for words, unable to come up with an excuse quickly enough to keep his ego from blowing up even bigger than it already was.

"Trust me, baby, I don't mind. Just don't embarrass yourself by being so loud that people can hear you even over the music."

"You're such a fucking nuisance, Nathan, I swear —what are you doing?" Bria questioned quickly as Nathan moved away to push his pants down.

"Taking my dick out," he stated simply. "Assuming you still want it...You do still want it, right?"

"Yeah!" Bria nodded quickly before clearing her throat and shrugging her shoulders. "I mean—Yeah," she murmured, trying to appear nonchalant.

Nathan rolled his eyes, an amused smile playing on his lips as he pulled his cock out and gave himself a couple of strokes. Bria's mouth fell open as she stared at it, but she quickly schooled her expression into something far less impressed as he looked at her.

"That's..." *a big dick*, she wanted to say, but she wasn't going to give him that satisfaction. "A dick," she settled for saying instead.

"Wow, look who took sex ed back in middle school," he gasped before pushing her to lie flat on her back again. He hovered over her, leaning down until his face was only inches away from hers, and Bria's eyes flickered between his and his lips as his breath fanned over her face. "Are you ready?" His usual taunting voice was replaced by a much gentler one as he stared at her seriously, waiting patiently for her response.

"Yes." She nodded before swallowing around the lump in her throat. "Just...Go slow, okay?"

"Of course," he murmured, hesitating for only a moment before leaning down to press a kiss against her lips. The kiss was gentle, their lips just barely touching, mouths just barely moving against each other.

Bria melted into it easily, wrapping her arms around his neck and pulling him even closer as she tilted her head to the side, letting out a soft whine as he poked his tongue inside of her mouth.

The kiss heated up rapidly, the two of their mouths moving together in perfect sync as they devoured each other hungrily, tongues tangling and teeth clanking together as their hands began to roam each other's bodies.

Bria ran her hands along Nathan's broad shoulders and muscular back as Nathan's large hand gripped her side, his fingers rubbing over her hip before clutching her thigh and then traveling back up her stomach to grab her breast.

Bria hardly registered the tip of Nathan's cock breaching her as she was overwhelmed by his roaming hand and his tongue as it explored her mouth, but she gasped, letting out a choked moan when she felt his length slipping farther inside.

The stretch stung for a couple of seconds, and she hissed, tensing up as she pulled away from their kiss, but Nathan quickly shushed her before moving his hand up to stroke her cheek.

"It's okay, I'm not gonna move yet," he whispered. "Just focus on me."

When Bria gave him a slight nod, Nathan leaned forward, taking her mouth in for another kiss, this one rougher than the last.

Maybe he had been waiting to do this for a little while. Every time she pissed him off—which just so happened to be every time he spoke to her—maybe he fantasized about kissing her to shut her up and then fucking her into oblivion after. Maybe.

Nathan hissed as Bria clenched around him and squirmed until he quickly grabbed her hip to stop her. "Don't," he gritted out, and Bria pulled away from their kiss, breathless and grinning.

"What? What's wrong?" She clenched again, and Nathan squeezed his eyes shut, trying not to pay attention to the way his cock throbbed and twitched inside her. The way his stomach tensed up as pleasure coiled up in the pit of it, much faster than it usually did. He couldn't remember the last time he'd felt this needy.

"Don't be a fucking tease," he growled.

"Or what?" she questioned, trying to squirm around again.

Nathan stared at her for a few moments before pulling back and thrusting forward again slowly. Bria bit her lip, trying not to react, and Nathan smirked as he realized that she was more than ready for the long overdue pounding that he'd always wanted to give her.

"You'll regret being such a bitch to me," he grumbled.

Bria opened her mouth to say something smart,

but the words died on her tongue as Nathan wrapped his arms around her thighs again, pushing her knees up toward her head before he began fucking her with no mercy. Bria's breath was just about knocked out of her as Nathan started up a quick pace, slamming into her with all the speed of a jackhammer as he held her firmly in place. She was practically bent in half as he leaned down to kiss her again, but the kiss was brief as he pulled away to look at her. He wanted to see her while he fucked her. He wanted to watch the way her face contorted in pleasure, her mouth falling open and eyebrows furrowing together as she moaned uncontrollably, even as she attempted to keep herself quiet.

Bria wrapped her arms around the backs of her thighs to hold her legs up, tears filling her eyes and blurring her vision as she tried to keep staring into Nathan's. It just felt so good—better than she ever could have imagined, and the pleasure was already overwhelming. The way she felt so full with his cock buried deep inside of her, the way he fucked her open and pounded directly into her G-spot with every thrust, the way he muttered filthy words in her ear as he pushed his fingers into her mouth, forcing her to suck on them...

"That's it." He smirked. "Good fucking girl. See?

I knew I'd like you better like this. On your back for me, with your little pussy being split open on my cock and your mouth too busy for you to say anything obnoxious. Even the brattiest of fucking brats can be tolerable, just as long as they're kept busy enough. Maybe I should fuck you like this all the time. I bet we'd get along better."

Bria gurgled and moaned around his fingers, and that was about as much of a response as she could give him as her eyes rolled into the back of her head before slipping shut. Nathan could tell by the way her pussy was spasming that she was close, and he was too after having to wait so long to have her.

He pulled his fingers out of her mouth, grabbing her jaw and shaking her head around until she opened her eyes again. "You look at me. Look me right in the eyes while you cum on my cock."

"Nathan," Bria whimpered. "Oh my God, I—oh my f-fuck, shit—"

"I thought you said I didn't know how to fuck a woman right?" Nathan taunted. "Doesn't seem like you feel the same way now. Say it. Say you love the way I fuck you."

"I—I love the way you—" Bria gasped, shuddering as he pushed both of her legs to one side of him. The new position was somehow a thousand times better, and Bria shook her head, tears slipping down her cheeks as she pressed her hand against his stomach. "I'm—it's too much, I'm gonna cum—"

"Not a second before you tell me how much you love the way I fuck you. Say it."

"I love it, I-I love the way you—I love the way you fuck me, please—"

"Go ahead." Nathan grinned. "And remember the way it felt to cum all over my cock the next time you decide to mouth off to me."

Bria wasn't listening, already several galaxies away as she convulsed underneath him, moaning and muttering about how 'fucking good' he was, amongst other slurred curses and nonsensical phrases.

Nathan held out for as long as he could, fucking her through her orgasm until she could do nothing more than tremble beneath him and let out the occasional, shaky moan, but when he was sure that she'd come down from her high, he quickly pulled out of her and began stroking himself, groaning and throwing his head back as he came all over her stomach.

He was aware that he probably looked like a maniac as he laughed in between groaning, smirking lazily down at the worn-out girl as he stared at her prettily painted stomach, but he didn't care.

"Been waiting to do that for a while," he stated cheekily, chest heaving as he attempted to catch his breath after the last of his seed had spilled over her stomach.

"Me too," she hesitantly admitted. "Glad...glad I lost my virginity to you. I guess."

"Yeah, any girl would be."

"Shut the fuck up."

# Dear Diary
Moran Fitzpatrick

Dear Diary,

You wouldn't believe the night I had!

And to think I'd been agonizing over the decision.

Do you remember how I told you that I had to choose between Tom and Ricky? Dating the two of them for the past few months has been amazing. I don't understand why they each had to go and ruin it by demanding that I choose.

As if I could possibly decide between the two....

Anyway, I'm glad that they pushed me to make a decision because I have had the best night of my life.

I want to write it all down so I can savor every exquisite detail.

Let me start at the beginning.

I'd been nervous as I sat across the table from Ricky. Up until a few moments earlier, he'd been sipping quietly on his drink, smiling over at me every so often. His green eyes had been alive and filled with humor when he arrived. He'd even stopped to rub my shoulders and give me a sweet kiss.

Soft music had been wafting from the speakers, punctuated by the occasional rise and fall of conversation. When the knots in my stomach had become too much for me to handle, I'd leaned back against the red vinyl booth and glanced around. With only a few people around us, the café had been largely quiet. Now and again, the group that had been sitting in the back laughed loudly, drawing our attention to them. Out of the corner of my eye, I'd noticed them glancing over at us, so I'd tossed my blond hair over my shoulders and straightened my back.

I'd known what they were thinking without asking.

Most of the time, whenever Ricky and I went out, we ended up getting the same confused looks, especially when we both stood up. Given that I was taller than Ricky and a lot louder, I'd grown used to being met with surprise.

Hell, I'd never even cared.

But I knew Ricky did.

So I'd let my eyes skim over the wooden tables lined up on either side of the cream-colored walls and paused at the tables scattered in the middle. Then I swung my gaze back to Ricky and lifted my lips into a slow, sensual smile.

"So what do you think?"

Ricky had cleared his throat and glanced down at his drink. "I don't know about this. This is a pretty big ask, Cal."

I'd shrugged and leaned forward against the table, offering him an obstructed view of my cleavage. In my knee-length yellow summer dress and tanned skin, I'd known that I had to use every tool at my disposal, including disarming Ricky with a dress that hugged my body in all the right ways.

He'd reacted the way I expected him to.

Even then, he hadn't been able to stop staring at me, a myriad of emotions dancing across his face. Unfortunately, I'd known from the second I walked in that it wasn't going to be easy. Getting Ricky to do what I wanted was one thing. Convincing him to engage in a threesome just so I could decide which man was a better fit was another.

And I'd had no way of knowing if either of them was going to say yes.

Considering Ricky's kind and docile nature, I'd known he'd be easier to win over. Having met him while I was picking up a shift at the bowling rink, the two of us had immediately hit it off. By the end of the night, he'd been all but ignoring his team and kept his eyes fixed solely on me.

It had been an intoxicating feeling.

You know the kind, diary.

As if I was drunk.

Last night hadn't been any different.

Ricky has a way of looking at me and making me feel like nothing else. Whenever he looked at me, it was like the world stopped turning, and I had to remind myself how to breathe. In spite of his serious and quiet nature, I knew what kind of man lurked underneath.

A thrill had raced through me at the thought of unleashing the beast within.

So much so that I'd continued to lean over the table until I took both of his hands in mine. He'd made a startled noise, but his eyes stayed on my face. I'd seen how much effort it took for him to hold completely still and refuse to answer my question altogether.

But I'd been determined to get my way.

A short while later, I'd stood up and wandered over to his side of the booth. As soon as I sat down, I'd placed a finger on his thigh and traced a path up. He'd sucked in a harsh breath when I'd leaned forward and palmed him.

"What are you doing?"

"Trying to make a case for myself," I'd replied breathlessly. "How am I doing so far?"

Ricky had struggled to swallow past the lump in his throat. "You do make a compelling case."

My fingers had given him another squeeze when he gasped, earning the attention of a uniformed waiter next to us. Ricky had offered him a tight, polite smile and turned his attention to the front. Quietly, he'd reached for his glass of water and downed it all in one gulp.

When he had finished his water, he reached for his soda.

Still, it hadn't deterred me.

On the contrary, it had made me want him even more.

He'd circled his fingers around my wrist and tugged. "I don't think is a good place for this."

I'd pouted. "But I want you."

Ricky had blown out a breath. "I want you too, but I'm not going to share you with anyone else."

"It's not sharing. Not in the long-term. It's just for a night."

Ricky had exhaled and linked his fingers together. "I just don't know if I'm comfortable with this arrangement. Why do you need this to prove something?"

I'd sighed and sat up straighter. "Because you're both amazing, and I want to have fun with both of you. There's no law that says I can't."

"No one said anything about a law."

I'd huffed, sat back, and crossed my arms over my chest. "So that's it?"

Ricky's expression had turned alarmed. "Now hang on a second—"

Before he'd finished his sentence, I'd been out of my seat, beaming. Tom Monroe had walked into the café and given me a mischievous grin before sweeping me into his arms. Once he'd set me down, I'd given him the once-over, starting with his ripped jeans, the shirt with paint splatters on it, and stopping at the shoulder-length brown hair falling in loose waves around his waves.

Tom had been looking especially hot.

I'd even considered dragging him off to the bathroom in the back, but I didn't want to leave Rick behind.

I'm stupid, aren't I, diary?

But then Tom's eyes had been studying me the entire time, bright blue and smoldering. "You look gorgeous."

And I'd melted into a puddle.

Have I mentioned how hot Tom is?

I'd beamed. "Thank you."

Suddenly, Tom had glanced over my shoulders at Ricky, who'd pressed his mouth into a thin white line. "What's up, Richard?"

"It's Ricky," he'd stressed with a lift of his chin. "What are you doing here?"

Tom had shrugged and thrown an arm over my shoulders. "Lie invited me."

"Lie," Ricky grumbled, underneath his breath. "I don't even know why."

"I invited him because this is about both of you," I'd said loudly. "I know you two don't like each other, but since I am seeing both of you, and you both want me to pick, I thought we should all talk about this like sane, mature people."

Ricky had snorted and sunk lower into his seat.

Then I'd removed Tom's arm from around my

shoulders and motioned from him to sit. He'd slid into the booth opposite Ricky and motioned to the waiter. Moments later, he'd given me a bright grin, making the butterflies in my stomach erupt.

Tom had his own kind of charm.

Where Rick was quiet and private, Tom was loud and full of life. The two of them couldn't have been more different, with the former preferring to spend his evenings at home, watching documentaries, and the latter spending his nights at poetry slams, strumming his guitar and writing in his notebook.

Since I hadn't been able to decide, I'd invited both of them to convince them of my plan. Given the amount of chemistry I had with the two of them, the only way to reach a satisfying conclusion was to sleep with the two of them.

At the same time.

Tom had brightened at the idea while Ricky slouched, some of the color draining from his face. Eventually, when I'd finally taken a seat, pulling a chair up with a screech and setting it at the head of the table, the two of them were sizing each other up.

"I think we should go back to my apartment and sort this out."

In silence, we'd made our way outside and into

the brusque evening air. Tom had taken my left side, a hint of spices and oranges clinging to his skin. Ricky, on the other hand, had smelled like sandalwood and sage, and he'd flanked my right side, brushing his hand against mine every so often.

A few blocks away, I'd led them up the stairs and stopped in front of the door.

I'd been so nervous, diary, I was sure I'd throw up then and there.

Instead, I took them inside and flicked the switch on and kicked off my shoes. By the time they'd settled on opposite sides of the couch, I'd peeled off my clothes and tossed them into a heap on the floor, leaving me in my red lace bra and underwear.

Ricky's mouth had fallen open.

Tom had leaned back against the couch, draping his arm over the back. "You look so sexy."

"Sexy enough for you to agree?" I'd sauntered over, stopping a few feet away. Then I'd given my hips a little extra sway before unhooking my bra. "I can't choose between the two of you, and this is the only way I know how."

Tom had shrugged and risen to his feet. "I'm down if you are."

With that, he'd pulled off his clothes, leaving him in his boxers. Moments later, he wandered over to me and tilted my head back. As soon as he kissed me, I'd thrown my head back, the knots in the center of my stomach unfurling. Tom had deepened the kiss, and my fingers linked over his head.

He sure did know how to take my breath away.

Warmth had pooled in the center of my stomach. Slowly, he'd leaned back to press hot, open-mouthed kisses along the side of my neck. His fingers had dug into my sides and pulled me against him. The length of him had brushed against me, and my knees had turned weak.

Until he'd lowered himself onto the floor and hooked a thumb underneath the waistband of my panties. His blue eyes had been bright and full of hunger as he slid them down over my legs and tossed them over my shoulders. Tom had pried my legs open and settled in between them, his mouth facing my center.

His tongue had darted in between my wet folds, sending me over the edge.

I'd wound my fingers through his hair and thrown my head back.

Tom had begun to make low, growling noises in the back of his neck when my eyes flew open. Out of the corner of my eye, I'd spotted Ricky getting up and taking off his shoes. His expression had turned relax, as if he was considering the whole thing more seriously. So I threw my head back and moaned. Tom's tongue continued to flick back and forth, stroking the bundle of nerves until I was shaking and panting his name.

As soon as I caught my breath, he'd stood up and kissed me soundly.

And so thoroughly I'd tasted myself on him.

Abruptly, he'd turned me around so I was facing Ricky. My eyes widened when he positioned himself behind me, and his arms came up on either side. He rubbed his hands up and down my arms while Ricky watched, his expression giving nothing away. Without warning, Ricky rose to his feet and peeled away his clothes. Once he was done, Tom entered me in one quick stroke.

I'd cried out his name so loudly I was sure the neighbors heard.

Over and over, we rocked back and forth against each other until my pulse quickened and a thin sheen of sweat broke out across my forehead. I threw my head back and wound my fingers through his hair. Tom sunk his teeth into my shoulders and made a low noise in the back of his throat that had shivers racing up and down my spine. When the force of my orgasm ripped through me, Tom had placed both hands around my stomach and squeezed.

He stayed inside of me until Ricky cleared his throat.

"Mind if I cut in?"

Tom had pressed a kiss to the back of my neck before easing out of me. With one last kiss, he strode over to the couch and lowered himself onto it. He spread his legs out on either side of him and stroked himself. Meanwhile, Ricky walked over to me and kissed me hard enough to make my toes curl. I'd swayed a little on my feet, the taste of soda and mint swirling around in my mouth.

When he drew back, he had the most intense look on his face.

With a wicked smile, I got down on my knees and kissed the tip of his member. Ricky made a low strangled noise, and his hands moved to the back of my head. He wound his fingers through my hair, drawing me closer to him.

I took him into my mouth and began to suck.

Ricky pumped in and out of my mouth, his face glistening with sweat. He dug his nails into my scalp and threw his head back. Moments later, I stopped and sat back on my legs. Then I stood up and cast a glance in Tom's direction. When I flipped my hair over my shoulders, I saw the two of them follow me.

It made me feel more powerful than I'd ever felt before, diary.

Like the two of them were going to fall to their knees and worship me.

With my heart hammering against my chest, I led them into my bedroom. Then I swallowed past the dryness in my throat, switched on the night lamp, and twisted to face them. I beckoned Ricky first and pushed him onto the mattress. I placed a leg on either side of him and cocked a finger in Tom's direction.

The bed dipped and creaked underneath him.

Tom placed his legs on either side of Ricky and glanced over my shoulders at him. A quick look passed between them before Ricky thrust upward. Moments later, when I was still adjusting on top of him, Tom thrust into me from the back.

Ricky's legs dangled over the edge of the bed.

As one, the two of them moved back and forth, easing out of me at an even, sensual pace. I threw my head back and squeezed my eyes, relishing every sensation that ricocheted through me. When Tom's hand came up around my breast, flicking the nipple, my hips bucked.

Then Ricky's hand went to the other breast, doing the same.

It wasn't long before my nipples were as hard as pebbles, and I began to bounce a little. Having both of them inside me at the same time was better than anything I could've imagined. Wave after wave of pleasure built up within me while I listened to the sound of their heavy breathing.

I don't think I've ever heard anything like that.

Once the smell of sweat and soap filled the room, my pulse quickened. I tried to keep my eyes open, to look at Ricky's handsome face, but I couldn't. Now and again, when I forced one eye open and saw the wild abandon on his face, I nearly collapsed on top of him. So I twisted my head to the side and stared at Tom, who gave me a heated look that had molten blood rushing through my veins.

I'd been expecting one of them to choke, or at the very least underperform under pressure. Unfortunately, not only were the two of them pounding into me like there was no tomorrow, but I was on the brink of another orgasm and still no closer to figuring out who was a better fit. Choosing based on who was better in the bedroom had seemed like a good idea at the time.

But all I'd been able to think about was how right

they both felt and how I wanted to stay like that until the world ended and our bones turned to dust. With wild and reckless abandon, the three of us moved together, moving closer and closer to an explosive climax.

Ricky tilted his head up and pressed his lips to mine.

I bit down on his bottom lip, and he growled.

Tom pressed both of my breasts together and sank his teeth into my neck. Dual waves of pain and pleasure rose within me, making my chest tighten. I curled my hands into fists on either side of the bed and blew out a deep, shaky breath.

The force of my third orgasm ripped through me, leaving me shaking violently. I writhed and spasmed, my lungs burning with effort. Tom gave a few more quick thrusts before pulling out and emptying himself onto the bed. Underneath, Ricky continued to thrust upwards, his thrusts growing harder and more frantic.

When he came, he jerked against me and went completely still.

Warmth pooled between my legs.

I rolled off of him and stared up at the ceiling.

Now, the two of them are sprawled on either side of the bed, with only a sheet to cover them. I'm hiding in the bathroom because I had to talk to someone, and I don't know who else to go to.

Last night didn't make anything clearer.

Instead, I'd discovered that they were both able to fuck me senseless.

So, diary, I think we're going to have to do it again a few times.

Just to be sure, you know.

# Watermelon
## Chrissy Lowell

"Are you sure about this?"

Kim sat up straighter and swung her gaze back to Kyle, who had a thin sheen of sweat on his forehead. He used the back of his hand to wipe his brow and blew out a breath. Then he stood up and after a few seconds of fanning himself, stripped off his shirt.

Revealing tanned and smooth muscles beneath.

Kim's mouth went dry. "Yeah, I'm sure. Why wouldn't I be?"

"Because it's a pretty big deal," Kyle replied with a slight shake of his head. "It's a pretty intimate thing."

Kim raised an eyebrow. "We've been together for two years, babe."

And she was more than ready to kick things up a notch.

As much as she loved Kyle, and the way he made her feel, she knew that they needed to try something different. While the sex between them still excited her and made her blood turn molten, they had been in a rut for a few months. Now and again, she found her mind wandering while he was on top of her, and she knew that something had to be done.

Which was why she had gone to Mary for help.

Usually, Mary was the one to talk her into doing crazy things, and over the years, Kim had learned to tune her out. Unfortunately, given the delicate nature of her situation, Kim knew she couldn't trust anyone else with this. Not when she had one shot to convince her sweet and nerdy boyfriend.

Kyle was eager to please her, and she took that as a good sign.

Slowly, she rose to her feet and dimmed the lights, casting the living room in a faint and eerie glow. Then she picked up her phone and issued a command, causing soft and sexy music to waft through the speakers overhead. In the distance, she heard the sound of tires screeching against asphalt and the howl of dogs, but she pushed it all away.

All she wanted was to focus on the man in front

of her.

He was sitting with his hands folded in his lap, barefoot on the carpet, and with his jeans hanging low on his hips. His dark, unruly hair was tossed to the side, giving him a vulnerable and more boyish look. Wordlessly, Kim stripped down to her underwear and bra. Kyle's eyes widened in surprise.

"Shouldn't we talk about this some more?"

Kim shrugged and kicked her clothes away. "We can, but there's no reason we can't be comfortable. Why don't you take off your jeans?"

Kyle chuckled. "I know what you're trying to do."

Kim's hips swayed as she wandered over to him. She sat down on the couch and swung around to face them. Her eyes never left his face as she stretched her legs out in front of her and lifted her arms up over her head.

Kyle couldn't look away from her.

"I'm not trying to do anything. I'm succeeding," Kim teased in a low and husky voice. "You're overthinking this. I'm trying to show you that you don't have to."

Kyle made a low noise in the back of his throat. "I don't want to hurt you."

Kim lowered her head and stared at him through

lowered lashes. "I want you to hurt me. There's a difference."

Kyle swallowed heavily. "What if you don't like it?"

"What if I do?" Kim sat up and crawled toward him, aware of his heated gaze making her skin crawl with anticipation. She stopped a few feet away and reached for his glasses. Carefully, she set them down on the table behind him, brushing herself against him as she did. Kyle stopped breathing and went still.

When she sat back down, he took several deep breaths. "What if I don't like it?"

"We'll stop then," Kim suggested, her tongue darting out to lick her lips. "But we won't know until we try."

Abruptly, Kyle stood up and unbuttoned his jeans. He pushed them down his ankles before kicking them off. As soon as he sat back down, her eyes fell to the bulge in his pants, straining against the fabric of his boxers. Her heart began to hammer inside of her chest, and a shiver of anticipation raced through her.

Was this it?

She pressed her back against the couch and brushed her hair out of her eyes. "Would it make you feel better if we had a safe word?"

Kyle paused and nodded slowly. "Yes."

"How about watermelon?"

Kyle threw his head back and laughed. "No offense, but it's a terrible safe word. Shouldn't you pick something else? Maybe something sexier."

Kim shrugged. "Why would I? This got your attention, didn't it? Besides, I like watermelons."

Although she doubted she was going to look at them the same after today.

Not that she minded.

Kyle stared at her for a few seconds before he covered the distance between them and kissed her. She sighed and linked her fingers over his neck. Before she could deepen the kiss, he drew back and ran a hand over his face.

"I want to tie you up," Kyle blurted out, his face turning a bright red. "I learned how to make knots when I was in the boy scouts...."

"I know."

"I'll make sure it's not too tight," Kyle added, his green eyes moving over her slowly, sensually. "I promise."

Kim nodded. "Okay."

Kyle searched her face. "There's still time to back out if you want to."

Kim stretched her entire body out on the coach

and smiled. "Not a chance. How do you want me?"

Kyle swallowed and stood up. "Just like that. Hold on. I'll be right back."

With that, he bolted to his feet and disappeared down the hallway. Kim could hear her heart pounding against her ears. She sat up, reached for her half-full glass of water, and gulped it down. Then she flipped onto her side and placed a hand on her hips, striking a suggestive pose.

Kyle wouldn't know what hit him.

As soon as he returned, the butterflies in her stomach erupted, and she resisted the urge to move. He knelt down in front of her and touched his mouth to hers. Kyle tasted like mint toothpaste. She made a low, whimpering noise in the back of her throat and pushed herself closer. Suddenly, her hand darted between them, and she gripped him over the fabric of his boxers.

He made a low, strangled noise and wrenched his lips away. "I want to fuck you for a while."

Kim's eyes widened. "Okay."

"If things are going too far..."

Kim shook her head. "They aren't."

Flipping the tables on her and taking charge was sexy.

The last thing she'd expected was for Kyle to

offer to tie her up. She had imagined him bending her over the couch and taking her then and there, without warning. By introducing rope into the mix, Kyle was heating things up, and it stoked something within her.

She had no idea he could be so domineering.

"Good." He motioned for her to sit up, and she did. The top of his head glistened underneath florescent lighting as he unwound his rope. His fingers moved quickly, deftly, like he had been doing this for a while. Before she knew what was happening, she found her feet firmly bound together. Then he took both of her hands in his and brought them up to his lips. Kyle took his time kissing each individual knuckle, letting his hot breath dance along the inside of her wrist before he sat back. With a wicked smile, he tied her hands together.

Kim tugged on the rope, and the low thrum in the center of her stomach turned molten. "I had no idea you were going to be this good."

"I had no idea you were going to look this sexy," Kyle replied in a husky voice. He knelt between them and nipped on her lower lip. She melted against him, fire rising up within her. When she parted her mouth to allow him access, Kyle's tongue slid in and began a sensual battle for dominance.

Every inch of her came alive.

She shifted, trying to pull him closer and pulled against her restraints. "Don't you want to come closer?"

Kyle's mouth moved down, pressing hot, open-mouthed kisses along the side of her neck. He stopped at her breasts and took one nipple between his teeth. Her pulse jumped when he licked and sucked until her hips bucked. Then he switched his attention to the other one, lavishing it with the same amount of attention so they were both as hard as pebbles.

Once he pulled back, Kim made a low, whimpering noise.

She burned for him.

His gaze was searing when he moved back to look at her. "Should I stop?"

Kim shook her head. "Never."

Abruptly, Kyle reached for her bound legs and threw them over his shoulders, so his mouth was at her center. He blew, his hot breath doing strange things to her insides. When his tongue darted out, in between her wet folds, Kim cried out. She threw her head back and cried out his name.

"I'm just getting started," Kyle promised in

between licks. He pressed his hands on either side of her and growled. "You taste amazing, Kim."

Kim gasped when his tongue began to swipe back and forth. "Oh, Kyle. Oh, yes."

"Yes what?"

"Yes, just like that."

"Like this?" Kyle gripped the edges of her feet and made a low noise in the back of his throat. He began to alternate between sucking her and licking back and forth, leaving her writhing and panting beneath him. She squeezed her eyes and ground against him, relishing every wave of pleasure that built up within her. Her eyes squeezed shut, and she dug her nails into the inside of her palms.

Wave after wave of pleasure rose up within her.

Sweat formed on the back of her neck and slid down the length of her back. Kyle's hands shifted, and he pressed her breasts together, sending another jolt through her. She made a low humming noise.

All at once, she was falling, the force of her pleasure ripping through her. Her eyes flew open, and spots danced in her field of vision. Kim's body writhed and spasmed while she gasped, her chest tightening with emotion. As soon as she could breathe again, her vision cleared, and Kyle lowered her legs. He knelt forward and kissed her, the taste of her juices strong on his lips. She sighed, and one arm traveled to the back of her neck, massaging the skin there. He framed her face in his hands, and his kiss turned gentle.

"Keep going," Kim pleaded breathlessly. "I don't want you to stop."

Kyle gave her another kiss before leaning back. He stood up and helped her to her feet. Then he swept her into his arms and took her into the kitchen. Slowly, he set her down on her feet and pulled out a chair with a screech. His heavy breathing reverberated inside of her head. With a smile, he brought the chair to a rest against the counter. Gently, he spun her around so her back was facing him. Her chest came to a rest against the front of the chair, her butt dangling off the edge of the seat.

He lowered himself onto the floor and untied her feet.

Without wasting any time, he tied her ankles to the feet of the chair. His breath was hot in her ear as he untied her hands and pulled them behind her back. In a few quick and nimble movements, he tied her wrists together and pressed a kiss between her shoulder blades.

Goosebumps broke out across her flesh.

She heard him suck a in harsh breath, and her

breath hitched in her throat. He ran his fingers down the length of her back and stopped at her behind. Then he used one hand to stroke the smooth skin there while the other messaged her scalp. Little pinpricks of desire burst through her, making her chest tighten.

"You have no idea how hot you are right now." Kyle's mouth moved over her flushed skin, leaving a trail of heat in his wake. He stopped when he reached the dip of her back and sat down. Moments later, she felt him brush himself against her, and her knees turned weak.

In one quick thrust, he was inside of her.

Kyle went absolutely still as her muscles contracted and expanded, taking in every inch of him. When she released a deep sigh, he began to move inside of her, his grunts and groans like music to her ears. The chair creaked and groaned underneath her. Through the thin walls of their apartment, she heard a TV, and the volume went up. Her lips lifted into a half smile as she shifted, trying to buck against him.

"Fuck, you feel so good, Kim." Kyle leaned forward and spoke directly into her ear, causing shivers to raise up and down her spine. "You're so tight and wet."

"I love being dominated by you," Kim said in a strangled voice. "Oh, Kyle. Oh, God."

He growled into her ear. "You like it when I'm dirty, don't you?"

"Yes," Kim ground out in between pants. "Oh, yes."

"Yeah, baby. You like it rough," Kyle continued in a voice that made the butterflies in her stomach erupt. "I like it when you beg for me."

"Oh, please."

Kyle eased out and slammed back into her. "Please what?"

"Please, Kyle." Kim squeezed her eyes shut, rivulets of sweat sliding down her back and the sides of her face. "Please don't stop."

Kyle made a guttural sound in the back of his throat. "I'm not going to stop. I could do this all night, baby."

"Yes," Kim breathed. "We should."

Kyle eased in and out of her in long, practiced strokes. First, he circled his hips, then he began to push upwards, hitting her sweet spot over and over. By the time another wave washed over her, Kim couldn't stop chanting his name. Her entire body shook and spasmed. He brought his head to a rest against her back and grew still. Then he untied her ankles and her arms.

She touched her wrists and spun around to kiss him, pouring every ounce of emotion she had into it. He responded by hoisting her up and carrying her into the bedroom. There, he set her down on the bed, his eyes staying on her face. Then he spun her around so her back was facing his and began to rub his hands up and down her arms. Then he tied her wrists together, giving the rope a firm tug before he moved down to her feet.

Without warning, he tied the left ankle to the right thigh and tied the left thigh to the left upper arm bicep. She twisted her head, and his lips found hers, soft and gentle. He moved his mouth against hers and shifted. When he turned her head to the front, she was facing the blue colored wall on the other side of the room.

Kyle eased into her from the back.

She blew out a breath. "This feels amazing."

Kyle kissed the back of her neck. "You're completely at my mercy."

"I am."

Kyle dug his fingers into her hips and circled. "Do you want me to go slow?"

Kim threw her head back and moaned. "Yes."

Abruptly, he slid out of her and slid back in again. "Are you sure about that?"

"I don't care. As long as you fuck me."

Kyle pressed a kiss between her shoulder blades, making the hairs on the back of her neck rise. "I love it when you talk dirty to me."

With a deep exhale, he buried his face in the crook of her neck and moved inside of her. She rocked back and forth against him, angling her body so he hit all the right spots. When his hands came up from behind and pushed her breasts together, she thought she was going to explode. Every part of her came alive and felt like it was on fire for him.

He flicked one nipple then the other.

Kim continued to stare at the spot on the wall and moan.

The bed creaked and groaned underneath him, the sound echoing in the stillness of the room. Kyle drew out of her and brought his hand to a rest against her hips. He slapped one butt cheek and the other before thrusting back in. Dual waves of pain and pleasure ricocheted through her. Her breathing turned into sharp little puffs as she struggled against her bindings.

"Don't cum yet," Kyle said directly into her. "I want you to hold it, Kim. Do you understand?"

She nodded. "I do."

He dug his nails into either side of her hips and pulled her against him. The smell of sweat and soap filled the room. He drew his mouth back, his hot breath dancing across her skin. When he sank his teeth into her shoulders, Kim jerked back and cried out. Kyle held her still against him and continued to pump into her, pushing her closer and closer to the edge.

Kim came undone with a violent spasm.

As soon as she regained her breath, Kyle gave a few quick thrusts, and warmth pooled between her legs. He went still against her, his breathing even. Slowly, his fingers moved over the rope, releasing her arms and legs. Once he did, she flipped onto her side and curled against him. With a smile, Kyle threw an arm over her shoulders and tucked her into his side.

"Where did you learn how to do that? The boy scouts definitely didn't teach you that."

Kyle chuckled and pressed a kiss to the top of her head. "Research. You've been dropping hints all week."

Kim looked up at him and smiled. "Want to show me more of that research?"

Kyle tilted her head back and kissed her. "We've got all night, baby."

# Wild Ella
## By Clifford Brannum

"You really went all-out tonight," Ella giggled, heat rushing up her cheeks. She peeled off her coat and draped it over her hand, her eyes darting around the candlelit room expectantly. "Are you sure your parents aren't going to come back?"

Caleb pulled her toward him. "They're out of town for the night. We have the house all to ourselves."

Ella tilted her head back, her blue eyes bright and mischievous. "Good."

Caleb claimed her mouth with his.

He'd been waiting a long time for this night.

She shuddered and melted against him, tasting like strawberry lip gloss and mint mouthwash. When she tilted her head to the side, he nipped on her lower lip, and her mouth parted.

His pulse quickened when her arms came up around his shoulders and squeezed.

All the blood rushed to his cock.

Slowly, Ella drew away from him and pushed her hair out of her face. "Why don't we get more comfortable?"

Caleb's heart hammered against his chest. "Sure."

With that, he led her toward the couch, barefoot over the wooden floorboards. He came to a stand in front of the couch and motioned for her to sit. Then he wandered over to the fireplace, bent down, and stoked the flames. They jumped and crackled, casting long, orange red shadows across the wall. Outside, the cold wind whistled and howled. Through the curtain, Caleb saw the crescent-shaped moon and smiled.

He was going to rock Ella's world, and she had no idea.

Not only were his parents gone for two whole days, but with the whole house to themselves and an excuse for Ella in place, the two of them were finally free to be together. He'd been dreaming about this night for months. Given that they'd been dating for an entire year, Caleb had done a good job of being patient, but he was about ready to explode.

And he wanted to lose himself in Ella.

She came up behind him, knelt down in front of the fire, and held up her hands. "I love this."

"I know how much you love fireplaces," Caleb murmured before pressing a kiss to her cheeks. "I also got us some wine."

Ella smiled and pressed her lips to his. "You really did think of everything."

Caleb stood up and pulled her to his feet. He wrapped his arms around her waist, and she tilted her head back to look up at him. "I want tonight to be special."

Ella blushed. "Me too."

As soon as he claimed his mouth with hers, she made a low whimpering noise and threaded her fingers through his hair. He couldn't believe how much he wanted her, needed to be inside of her. One hand stayed on her waist, and the other traveled up, stopping at the back of her neck. He kneaded the muscles there, and she shivered.

Holy shit.

He couldn't wait to feel every inch of her skin pressed against his.

Impatiently, he maneuvered them backwards

until they reached the couch. Ella lowered herself onto it with a low, whimpering sound. Reluctantly, he wrenched his lips away and pulled his shirt up over his head. With a smile, he tossed it over his shoulder and waited till it fell with a flutter. Ella fumbled with the zipper on the front of her hoodie.

Caleb sat down and helped her, letting the tight fabric fall behind her.

In the soft light, her skin glistened, and she had a warm glow around her. Caleb's heartbeat quickened as he reached for her and framed his face in her hands. She kissed him back slowly, gently, as if they had all the time in the world. One hand stayed on the back of her neck, and the other moved up and down her arms, leaving a trail of heat in its wake.

Ella drew him closer.

Once she fell backwards against the couch, Caleb draped himself over her, her bra the only barrier between them. He ran his fingers along her tan, smooth skin and stopped at the hook. Her mouth parted when he fumbled with it, managing to get it undone after some grunting. Abruptly, she sat up, pressed her arms together, and pulled it off.

His eyes moved over her face before sliding down to her breasts.

Round, perky, and full.

Just like they always were.

Caleb's mouth watered as Ella lowered herself back onto the couch and pushed her dark hair out of her eyes. Her lips spread into a slow, sultry smile, and all of his blood rushed south. In the back of his throat, he made a guttural sound before lowering his head. He took one nipple between his teeth and tugged.

She tasted like butter and vanilla.

His eyes rolled to the back of his head as she moaned, linking her fingers behind his neck. She wrapped her legs around his waist as he moved to the other breast and pinned her arms over her head. Ella's gasp of surprise made his cock twitch. He rubbed himself against her, and she bucked, a thin sheen of sweat breaking out across her forehead.

"Shit. You have no idea how badly I want to fuck you right now," Caleb breathed, pausing to blow out a breath. "I can't wait to be balls deep inside of you."

Ella's eyes flew open, and she stared at him through lowered lashes. "I want you too, Caleb."

His fingers moved to the zipper of her jeans. "Let me get these damn clothes off."

Ella took her hand in his and sat up. "Not like this."

Caleb glanced up at her. "What do you mean?"

"I want to wait till I'm married, remember?"

"You're joking, right?"

"No, I've been telling you for months. I wasn't trying to be sexy or playing hard to get. I want to be a virgin when I get married."

Caleb frowned. "So what are we going to do?"

"We can still have fun, Caleb," Ella replied with a smile. "Okay?"

"Okay."

Ella palmed him over the thin fabric of his jeans and squeezed. "You don't sound convinced."

Caleb rubbed himself against her. "I just want you so badly."

Ella covered the distance between them and kissed him hard. "You can still have me."

Caleb growled into her mouth, "I want to fuck you, Ella. And I know you want to fuck me too."

Ella made a low choking noise and pressed herself against him. Caleb moved his hands up and down her bare arms, leaving goosebumps in his wake. He dug his nails into her waist, and she murmured his name. Suddenly, Ella drew back and stood up. Her eyes never left his face as she unbuttoned her jeans and slid them down her legs. Once they pooled at her ankles, she stepped out of them, revealing lacy black underwear underneath. Caleb's mouth fell open when she spun around, bent over, and pulled her underwear down over her tight, toned ass.

She wheeled back around to face him. Caleb had dug his palms into the couch, his erection straining painfully against his boxers. Wordlessly, Ella came to stand in front of him, completely naked, placed one leg on either side of him, and settled on his lap, the smell of her sweet juices wafting up his nostrils. Caleb placed a hand on her waist, and the other brushed her hair out of her face.

"Tell me what you want, baby," Caleb whispered into her skin.

Ella ground against him. "I want to feel you."

Caleb lifted his hips up off the couch and rubbed himself against her. "How's this?"

Ella threw her head back and moaned, the sound echoing in his ears. "Fuck, that feels so good."

Caleb placed his other hand on her waist and squeezed. "How about now?"

Ella blew out a breath. "You feel so good."

Caleb buried his face in her neck and breathed. "Fuck, Ella. I don't know how to control myself around you."

Ella lifted herself up and ground against him, harder this time.

His cock pulsed and twitched.

Ella linked her fingers through his hair and drew his head back. She pressed him against her chest and bounced up and down. He squeezed his eyes shut and took a nipple between his teeth. Caleb's mouth darted between the two until they were both as hard as pebbles. As soon as they were, his hand darted between them and slipped in between her slick, wet folds.

Her juices immediately coated his hand.

She cried out and bucked against him.

He pushed another finger in and wasted no time finding her sweet spot. Ella dug her fingers into his shoulders and rocked against him. The couch creaked and dipped underneath them. Ella came a short while later, writhing and spasming against him. Her muscles expanded and contracted while his fingers continued to move. Once she caught her breath, he removed his fingers and looked at her.

As soon as her eyes cleared, he placed both fingers in his mouth and sucked. "You taste good."

Ella leaned between them and pressed her lips to his. "So do you."

Caleb swallowed. "What now?"

On shaky legs, Ella stood up and gathered her hair up off the nape of her neck. "You can get rid of those clothes."

Caleb was on his feet in an instant and pulling at his jeans. They fell to the floor with a flutter, joining the pile of clothes there. His hands were clumsy and sweaty as he pulled his boxers down and stood up to face her. Ella's eyes traveled over him, starting at the top of his head and stopping at his enlarged manhood. She paused, and her eyes widened slightly. When her tongue darted out to lick her lips, Caleb balled his hands into fists at his sides.

Although the evening was not going how he'd hoped, Caleb knew he wouldn't want to be anywhere else. Especially when Ella approached him and knelt down on the carpeted floor. On her knees, she sat back on her legs and looked up at him. Slowly, she leaned forward so her mouth was inches away from his member.

Ella began to lick him, and he growled, "Yes, baby. I love how your mouth feels on me."

She made a noise of agreement in the back of her throat and placed one hand on either side of his thighs. Quickly, she shifted so she took all of him. Her tongue moved quickly and deftly, bringing him closer and closer to the edge. He cupped the back of her neck and squeezed firmly. Ella glanced up at him and stopped. Suddenly, he pulled her to her knees, and she pressed herself against him.

"I want to be inside of you," Caleb told her, dark eyes moving intently over her face. "I know you want to be a virgin, and I respect that, but I need to be inside of you or I'm going to go crazy."

Ella nodded and kissed him.

Before he could deepen the kiss, Ella turned around and bent over so her ass was in the air. She looked over at him and gave him a wicked smile that made the blood on his veins pound. He stroked her back and licked his mouth.

"I want you to fuck me in the ass," Ella told him in a husky voice.

"What?"

Ella wriggled against him, her smile growing wider. "I know you've thought about it. Don't you want to have fun?"

Caleb cleared his throat. "Well, yeah, but isn't it kind of painful?"

Ella shook her head. "Not if you do it right."

Caleb positioned himself behind her and stopped. "Are you sure?"

"There's some water-based lubricant in my bag," Ella replied, swinging her gaze back to the front. "It'll help."

Caleb took a few steps back and fumbled in the semi-darkness until his hand closed around her backpack. In the front pocket, he found the tube and held it up to the flickering light. He squeezed a generous amount onto his finger and went to stand behind Ella. Using two fingers, he rubbed the lube all over himself, his fingers slick and clumsy. Ella was already touching herself and moaning.

Uncertainly, he came to stand behind her and thrust forward. "I don't think it's working."

Ella twisted her arms behind her back, stopping a few inches away from his member. "Can you see it?"

Caleb peered at her behind. "Yes."

"You have to aim for it," Ella murmured in a hoarse voice. "Can you do that?"

Caleb cleared his throat and tried again, but he kept missing. He made a low, frustrated noise and stepped back. "I don't think I can do this."

Ella craned her neck over her shoulders and smiled at him. "Yes, you can. I'll help you."

Caleb smirked. "I wasn't aware you were such an expert."

Ella chuckled. "I'm not, but I know my way around. Okay, can you see me properly?"

"Yes."

"Position yourself behind me and ease in," Ella

instructed, her voice rising toward the end. "Don't go in all at once."

Caleb blew out a breath, took a few steps forward, and did as he was told. When the tip went in, he went still and cursed. "Fuck, that feels so good."

"We're just getting started," Ella promised in a throaty voice. "Now ease out of me and slam back in."

Caleb gripped her hips, eased out, and thrust back in. "Like this?"

Ella bucked against him, and her head twisted to the front. "Exactly."

With a grunt, Caleb dug his nails into her waist and rocked back and forth against her. She bucked against him, mumbling incoherently into the darkness. Suddenly, she twisted to face him, and the look on her face nearly had him exploding. Ella licked her lips and cleared her throat.

"I want you to go in deeper," Ella whispered. "Keep thrusting in and out of me, but each time, go deeper."

Caleb grunted in agreement and sucked in a deep breath. Over and over, he thrust in and out of her, pushing himself farther in each time. As soon as he was all the way in, Ella went completely still and let out a deep, shaky breath. Suddenly, she began to grind against him with wild and reckless abandon.

He brought his head to a rest against her glistening, flushed back. "You're so tight, Ella. Fuck."

"Oh, Caleb. You're so big." Ella threw her head back and moaned. Out of the corner of his eye, he saw her hand move and dart in between her wet folds. His blood began to roar in his ears when he heard the familiar sounds of her pleasure reverberating inside of his head. Abruptly, Ella's hand darted out, and she placed one hand on either side of her thighs.

Caleb stood up straighter and circled his hips. "Is this how you want to be fucked?"

Ella let out a deep, throaty moan. "Oh, yes."

Caleb's nails dug into her waist, keeping her in place. "Good because I want to keep fucking you, Ella. I hope you're ready because we're going to be up all night."

"Oh, Caleb."

"That's it," he coaxed roughly. "That's a good girl."

"Harder," Ella pleaded in a strangled voice. "Please."

Caleb brought his head to a rest against the small

of her back and blew out a breath. "You're not so innocent, are you? You like it dirty, don't you, Ella?"

Ella cried out his name. "I like you fucking me."

Caleb growled into her back, "Good because I plan on doing this all the time."

Ella bit back her whimper.

"Don't hold back," Caleb said, drawing back. His hands moved forward, and he played with her nipples. "I want to hear you. I want to hear you while I'm fucking you, Ella."

"The neighbors," Ella gasped when his hand came up over her center and squeezed. She bucked against him and began to chant his name. He pushed one finger then another and thrust into her. Ella rocked back and forth against him, her movements wild and reckless. Together, the two of them moved, inching closer and closer to the edge.

Caleb squeezed his eyes shut and enjoyed the feel of her, pulsing and writhing around him. She was tight and wet and much better than anything he'd imagined. He soon found her sweet spot, and he stroked. When she began to moan, he pressed his face against her back and grunted.

She came undone with a violent shudder, rocking and spasming against him. He held her still while she rode out her high, his rhythm turning slow and pronounced. Ella caught her breath as he held her up by her ass and thrust deeply inside of her. She gasped and held still.

He eased in and out of her in long, practiced strokes.

Ella ground against him, the sound of her whimpers like music to his ears. Eventually, she twisted her arms over her back and reached for him. He leaned into it and pressed his lips together. She wound her fingers through his hair and tugged, sending dual waves of pain and pleasure in quick succession.

Her cries echoed off the walls, making the blood in his veins boil.

Suddenly, his entire body seized and jerked. He groaned, pouring himself into her while she stroked his hair. Ella was panting and still as he rode out his high. Once his breath returned to normal, she shifted, and he eased out of her. She drew him into her arms and held him to her as they both shuddered.

Slowly, she leaned back to looked up at him. "How was it?"

Caleb gave her a weak smile and kissed her forehead. "You have to teach me more."

Ella chuckled. "You got it."

# Christine's First Gangbang
## By Richard Kinney

"I can't believe this is actually happening!" Christine squealed, bouncing up and down as she clapped her hands together. "Thank you so much, Matt, really! You're the best!"

"I am," Matt agreed easily, smirking as he wrapped an arm around her waist and pulled her close to prevent her from running inside just yet. "Now promise me that you'll remember my one and only rule for the night."

"Of course, I promise." Christine nodded quickly. "The last man who gets to cum inside me tonight... will be you."

"Good girl." Matt leaned down to plant a kiss on her lips, patting her behind a few times before opening the door for her. "Let's go."

Christine giggled, smiling so widely that her cheeks were beginning to get sore as the two of them walked inside.

Matt had finally agreed to bring her to the sex club that they'd been hearing rave reviews about for the longest time, and Christine was already over the moon with happiness! She'd always wanted to pay a visit to a sex club, but before she'd started dating Matt, she'd never had anyone that she felt safe enough with.

Thankfully, she and Matt had managed to build a relationship filled with trust and mutual respect, so she was completely comfortable being here with him tonight, and he was fully comfortable with helping her finally fulfill her long-time dream of getting gangbanged.

It had been one of Christine's biggest fantasies for as long as she could remember—being surrounded by cocks, manhandled, used like nothing more than a fuck toy by men that she didn't even know—but she hadn't been able to make it happen until now, and it was all thanks to Matt.

He'd been a little iffy about it when she'd first told him that it was something that she wanted to try, but the more he thought about it, the more he liked the idea of watching his girlfriend being used by men that he got to handpick himself. He was a bit of a sadist, not to mention a voyeur, so this was right up his alley.

Besides, Christine had an insatiable hunger for sex, and as much as he hated to admit it, sometimes Matt found himself struggling to keep up. But if all went well tonight, the two of them would be making frequent trips back to the sex club, and Christine would be able to wear herself out with a whole flock of cocks as often as she pleased. This was a win for them both.

The inside of the club was lively and somewhat intimidating to newcomers like themselves. The first thing they saw upon walking in was several women in cages around the room, some of them masturbating, some of them pole-dancing, all of them naked. There were velvet couches all around. Some people sat watching the women perform, others seemed to be participating in one giant orgy.

Matt's cock twitched as his eyes trailed the large room for a few seconds before he forced himself to look away in order to locate the hallway that led to the more private rooms.

There were still plenty of people inside, they

noticed once they walked inside of one, but there were significantly fewer people than there were in the main area.

Matt wore a proud smile as heads turned and eyes caught on the beautiful woman that was standing next to him. Christine was drop-dead gorgeous, if you asked him. Her long, wavy blond hair, green eyes, and petite yet curvy body always seemed to draw attention wherever they went, and tonight, she was only wearing an all-black lingerie set, having decided to forgo picking out an outfit when she knew it'd only be ripped off her anyway.

She looked like a model, and Matt could tell by the way some of the men perked up and eyed her curiously that they were interested in getting a piece of her.

Perfect.

Matt took his time scanning the room, trying to find just the right men for the job. When he caught sight of a group of five big, muscular men who all seemed to be eye-fucking Christine as they pointed and talked about her, he grabbed her hand and began dragging her over to them, wearing an easy smile as he approached them.

"Hey." He tried not to sound so awkward as he

sent them a wave. "I'm Matt, and this is my girlfriend, Christine."

"Hey," one of them greeted, licking his lips as he eyed the suddenly shy-looking girl, who was trying her best to hide behind Matt's back, though he pulled her to stand in front of him once he noticed.

"Would any of you guys happen to be up for a gangbang tonight?" Matt decided to just cut straight to the chase. "Christine doesn't mind begging if you guys are into that, but if not, we can find some other guys–"

"No, no, no, we're definitely into it," one of them chuckled. "I think it's safe to say that we'd all be down for a gangbang. I'm Liam, by the way, and this is Dean, Nolan, Colton, and Dominic–not that it matters much, huh?" He smirked as he eyed Christine, his eyes catching on her small breasts for a moment before trailing back up to her face. "So Christine is a free-use slut and you're like her owner, right?"

Christine's cheeks turned bright red as she turned to look at Matt, who was no stranger to the obvious look of arousal swirling around in her eyes. He let out a fond chuckle, squeezing her hip with a bruising grip as he looked at the guys and nodded.

"Yeah, that sounds about right."

"Nice," Dean said, gesturing for them to follow him toward a nearby couch. "So anything we should know before we start? Any rules and boundaries to keep in mind?"

"There isn't much that she doesn't like." Matt shrugged his shoulders. "She likes it rough. Choking, slapping, hair-pulling, spitting, spanking, biting, scratching–the whole nine. Do whatever you want, but her safe word is 'Gymnastics,' and if she can't talk, she'll tap you six times if she wants you to stop. Oh–and try to keep all her holes filled at all times. She gets whiny when she's empty for more than a couple of seconds. Here–do you mind if I watch from the couch while you guys fuck her on the floor? It's where she belongs anyway."

"No problem," Nolan said, already tugging her panties off. The rest of them were already naked–another reason why Matt had decided to go up to them. They were all hung. "Is she already prepped and stretched?"

"Yep." Matt grinned. "She was so excited to come here today that she spent a couple of hours getting herself ready last night. She looked so cute begging for me to fist her."

"Fisting?" Liam raised his brows, eyeing the girl who was now being fondled by Colton and Dean.

The two of them both had one of her breasts in hand, squeezing them as Nolan kicked her legs apart and pushed three fingers inside her cunt.

"She's sturdier than she looks," Matt stated simply, yanking down his sweats before taking a seat on the couch.

Christine's eyes fluttered shut as she listened to her boyfriend talking about her as if she wasn't even there. She was already dripping wet, which Nolan commented on with a quiet chuckle as he pulled his fingers out of her cunt and pushed them inside of her mouth. She opened her eyes again, staring at him as she sucked on his fingers eagerly, and the men surrounding her hooted and laughed as they repositioned her, putting her on her knees.

"I want her mouth first. She looks like she gives good blowjobs," Colton commented.

"How come you always get to have first dibs?" Dominic grumbled under his breath.

"Oh, yeah, I forgot to mention, don't hesitate to share one hole between two cocks," Matt chuckled. "She can handle it."

"Wow, we really lucked out tonight," Liam murmured as he pranced over to them, wordlessly sliding down to the ground and pushing Christine's knees apart. He lay down on his back, wrapping his arms around her thighs and pulling her down until she was sitting on his face, and she gasped as his tongue immediately began trailing between her folds.

Matt began stroking himself slowly as he watched Colton grab Christine's hair and pull her head forward. She dutifully opened her mouth, easily welcoming his large girth inside. He moved his hips slowly, pushing his cock all the way to the back of her throat before pulling out until only the tip of it was still inside her mouth. Dominic pushed the tip of his cock inside as well, clearly surprised by the fact that she was able to fit them both.

"Holy shit," Dean groaned as he tilted his head. "Look how pretty she looks with two cocks in her mouth...Where did you find a girlfriend like this?!"

"I guess I lucked out as well," Matt chuckled.

Christine moaned, grinding against Liam's face as she stared up at the two men with their cocks in her mouth. Her jaw was already starting to ache, and her lips burned from being stretched so wide, but she loved the feeling. She loved the way her drool leaked from her mouth and over her exposed breasts too. When the two of them both pulled out, she furrowed her brows in confusion until Dominic pushed his entire length back inside before pulling out and allowing Colton to do the same.

The two of them started up a steady rhythm, taking turns fucking her face as she held her mouth open and tried her best not to gag around their massive cocks. Meanwhile, Liam was still eating her out like a man that had been starved. Christine's eyes rolled back as he made her continue to slide back and forth over his face, tongue-fucking her quickly. She was already quivering as her first orgasm of the night rapidly approached.

She was always quick to cum, so Matt wasn't surprised to see her trembling through an orgasm just a couple of minutes later, the lower half of Liam's face soaked once he pulled himself off from under her with a pleased smile.

Just a few minutes after that, Colton and Dominic reached their peak too. Colton shoved his cock into her mouth one final time, ordering her not to swallow until they gave her permission as he came down her throat. Dominic managed to hold out until he was finished, but the moment Colton pulled out, Dominic began stroking himself quickly, groaning as he watched his seed land all over Christine's tongue.

"Shit," Nolan mumbled as he stared at her, watching as some of the cum dripped off her tongue and onto the ground, but she still held her mouth open as she'd been told to. It wasn't until after both Colton and Dominic had spit inside her mouth that they gave her permission to swallow, which she did, happily. The sight drew a low groan out of Nolan, who immediately called next dibs on her mouth.

Liam grabbed Christine by her hair, forcing her to crawl behind him as he walked over to Dean. "Why don't the two of us share her ass and pussy while Nolan uses her mouth?"

"You know I'm not going to say no to that," Dean chuckled, pulling Christine up by the arm. "You get behind her, I'll get in front."

Liam nodded wordlessly, spinning the girl around until she was facing away from him and pressed against Dean. She gasped, letting out a startled squeak as he hiked one of her legs up until Dean rested the palm of his hand beneath her thigh to hold it up himself. Liam pushed down on her back, forcing her to arch it and lean closer to Dean while he pressed the head of his cock against her ass hole.

Christine bit her lip as he slid inside in one quick motion. She was hardly used to the feeling of his large cock stretching her ass when Dean slipped inside of her cunt, letting out a slew of curses as he felt her warm heat wrapped around his cock.

"Oh my God," she practically whispered as she clung to Dean, resting her forehead against his shoulder as the two of them began slowly thrusting in and out of her. She didn't get to rest there for long before her body was being twisted slightly and she was forced to bend forward until she was face to cock. Nolan tapped the tip of his cock against her lips until she opened her mouth and welcomed him inside.

The position was uncomfortable for Christine, whose muscles were already starting to sting and burn, but she didn't mind it if it meant getting to please three different cocks at once–four when Dominic came over to get a handjob after getting it up again.

Christine was overwhelmed as Dean and Liam took turns pounding into her quickly. Her ass was still sore from yesterday when Matt had fisted her, and her pussy was already sensitive from her first orgasm, so she was already feeling thoroughly used. On top of that, she was hyperaware of the fact that her own boyfriend was watching her as she was shared between the large men, and he wasn't the only one watching. She could feel the stares of the other people in the room burning into her skin as they all watched, getting themselves off while they did.

Matt was aware of it too. He couldn't wipe the smug expression off his face as he eyed the twenty or so other men in the room while they stared in awe at his girlfriend. It seemed to be an unspoken rule not to impose on a scene that you hadn't been asked to be a part of, so none of them approached her, which Matt was grateful for. But he could see how badly they wanted to join in on the fun, and he was already taking note of who he'd like to see fuck her next time.

Christine was preoccupied enough as it was for now, though, and Matt quickly turned his attention back to her when he heard her muffled moans becoming more frequent. Like clockwork, she came after just a couple of minutes, and the men continued fucking her afterward, even as she tried to squirm away from them. Nolan emptied his load inside her mouth a few minutes later, and she swallowed every drop of his cum just as eagerly as she'd swallowed Colton's and Dominic's earlier.

Dean was next to cum, pulling out of her cunt in order to paint her face with his seed instead, but when Liam came, he remained balls deep inside her ass, making sure that not a drop of it slid out until he pulled out of her and allowed her to collapse to the ground, free for someone else to use next.

Dominic and Colton both decided to share her cunt. Dominic was already close because of the handjob that she'd given him, but he'd been holding out just so he could have the chance to fuck her gaping cunt, and Colton wasn't about to miss out on the chance to double penetrate someone when he'd never had the opportunity to do so before, so he was quick to slide in alongside Dominic.

Christine cried out as her pussy was stretched while she slowly sank down on the two of their cocks. She barely had the strength to move by that point, and it was all she could do to hold herself up while the two of them pounded into her quickly. Colton grabbed her hand and forced her to rub her clit even as she cried and whined about being too sensitive to touch herself, chuckling as she sniffled and sobbed while slowly rubbing circles over the swollen nub.

Matt had stopped touching himself long ago, and now he was clutching the base of his cock tightly to keep himself from cumming untouched as he watched. He'd majorly underestimated just how hot getting to watch this would be. At this point, he couldn't believe that there had ever been a time when he'd been hesitant to agree to this, even if it was brief.

Christine ended up squirting twice before Colton and Dominic came, and by the time the two of them pulled out in order to cum all over her stomach, she could hardly find the strength to move, but she pulled herself to sit up with a look of determination on her face anyway. She had made a promise, after all.

Matt crooned at her, smiling as she gingerly crawled over to him and climbed into his lap with a quiet groan. "Your turn," she murmured, already burying her face in the crook of his neck sleepily.

Matt easily slid inside her loose cunt, letting out a sigh of relief as he finally got to be inside of his girlfriend for the first time tonight. "Such a good girl," he complimented, stroking her hair as he fucked into her with shallow thrusts. "You were a star tonight! You know you look gorgeous while you're pleasing a bunch of cocks, right?"

Christine grunted, and that was as much of a response as Matt was going to get. He chuckled as he squeezed her closer to him, hugging her as he continued fucking her sloppy cunt until he came.

He was smug as he spilled inside of her, satisfied by the longing looks on everyone else's faces. He was the only one who had the privilege of cumming inside of her pussy, and the only one who ever would. It was a reminder, for him and for her and for everybody else as well, that no matter how many other men she fucked, she would always truly belong to him and him only.

# The Massage
By Marine Leland

"Fuck," Sherry practically mewled, her body melting into the mattress as her muscles finally relaxed for what felt like the first time in centuries. "Right there! Fuck, yes, that feels so good!" she moaned when Lucy's fingers began digging into the right side of her neck.

"Sherry," Lucy giggled as she tried to fight off the blush that was threatening to cover her cheeks. She was thankful that Sherry was lying face down, unable to see what a flustered mess she was becoming. "I've barely even touched you yet!"

"Yeah, but your fingers are literally magical!" Sherry fussed in between moans. "I've been here for like three minutes, and already my body feels like a cloud. I haven't felt this light since I was a ten-year-old without a worry in the world aside from how to convince my mom to buy me my fifth Barbie lunchbox of the school year. Why have you been keeping your hidden talent a secret from me, your supposed best friend?!"

"You're so dramatic." Lucy snorted. "And is a hidden talent really a hidden talent if it's not a secret? Telling people about it defeats the whole purpose. Besides, every time I mention that I'm good at giving massages, people start expecting them from me all the time. My biggest mistake in life is telling my sister's big, dumb boyfriend about the massage therapy classes I took a few years ago. Now I'm stuck working the kinks out of his hairy back every other weekend unless I want to hear my sister's guilt-tripping."

"No, I'd say your biggest mistake in life was telling me about the massage therapy classes." Sherry grinned after lifting her head and turning to look back at Lucy. "Now I'm gonna have to test your knowledge. Thoroughly. I'm thinking we'll have to schedule a couple of sessions per week. Three massages at the minimum!"

Lucy smirked and pushed Sherry's head back

down without a word. She wasn't quite sure what to say to that. It wasn't as if she'd mind it if they really made that a thing anyway. If it meant having Sherry sprawled out on her bed, completely naked aside from a thin towel spread over her behind more often, then Lucy was all for it...

Lucy bit her lip as she stared down at Sherry. Her pale skin was shiny from the massage oil that Lucy had rubbed all over her before officially getting started with her massage, and her ass cheeks were poking out from underneath the tiny towel.

Lucy tried her best not to ogle Sherry's body, clearing her throat as she grabbed the bottle of oil and poured some more into the palm of her hand.

"I'm just gonna..." She drifted off, awkwardly straddling Sherry's behind before beginning to rub her neck and shoulders again.

"Shit," Sherry moaned as soon as Lucy's fingers came in contact with her skin again, and Lucy swallowed thickly, mentally scolding herself for the way her body reacted to the sound. Her hole clenched without her permission, her panties growing damp as she listened to her friend's satisfied moans.

As she worked her way down Sherry's back, Sherry's moans only grew even louder, breathier, needier. Lucy had given enough massages to be able to do it without having to pay much attention, so she allowed her mind to drift elsewhere as she continued kneading Sherry's flesh, but that was the worst thing that she could have possibly done.

Filthy images flashed through her mind as she wondered what else could make Sherry moan that way. She pictured Sherry lying among a pile of soft, fluffy pillows and blankets, blue eyes rolled into the back of her head as Lucy played with her breasts, fondling them, pinching and pulling on her nipples, sucking hickeys onto the plump flesh.

She pictured herself and Sherry lying side by side, facing each other, limbs tangled together as they stuck to each other like glue. Sweaty skin rubbing together as they exchanged a sloppy kiss and rolled their hips in a steady rhythm, cunts bumping against each other with every movement.

She pictured Sherry on top of her, sitting on her face, riding her tongue with her head thrown back, mouth wide open and hands cupping her breasts as she moaned so loudly that Lucy's neighbors would be able to hear it.

Lucy let out a quiet moan too, and then a gasp as she realized that she'd started moving, rolling her hips back and forth as she tried to grind her cunt against Sherry's behind.

Her cheeks felt as if they were on fire as she held her breath, staring at the back of Sherry's head, trying to figure out whether she'd noticed or not. It didn't seem that she had because she was still moaning, still whimpering, still mumbling about how good Lucy was.

Lucy could hardly breathe as she slowly moved back, straddling Sherry's legs in order to focus on Sherry's thighs instead. She hesitated for only a moment before her fingers dug into the tender flesh.

Lucy was practically drooling as she rubbed the back of Sherry's thigh, the smooth skin warming quickly under her touch. She tried to distract herself by looking around her bedroom rather than staring directly at Sherry's perfect skin, but there wasn't a hope that she could get her mind out of the gutter now. Every time she closed her eyes, all she could see was Sherry in one vulgar position or another, moaning and convulsing as she reached her completion.

Lucy's fingers traveled from the back of Sherry's thigh to the inside of it, and Sherry gasped, tensing up as Lucy's fingers disappeared underneath her towel, between her legs, and dangerously close to her cunt.

"Sorry!" Lucy apologized quickly, but Sherry merely lifted her behind, wiggling it from side to side for a moment before turning to look back at Lucy.

"No, you're fine, I'm just a little sensitive there," she giggled. "You can continue, but, ugh...If your fingers are gonna be so close to my cunt, then this massage better have a happy ending." She winked.

Lucy's eyes widened, and her mouth fell open as she choked out a surprised laugh and tried to figure out how to respond. She knew that Sherry was probably just joking around, but she also had the urge to scream at the top of her lungs, "Yes! Please let me give you a happy ending!"

Instead, she opened and closed her mouth like a fish, nodding before shaking her head before nodding again.

Sherry watched Lucy's glitching with an amused smile and a mischievous look in her eyes. "If I didn't know any better, Lucy, I'd say that you want me."

Only a blind fool could be oblivious to Lucy's constant staring, the way her fingers roamed a little too much, the way she stuttered and blushed whenever Sherry did or said...Well, anything. Sherry was well-aware of her friend's attraction to her. She was hoping that Lucy would finally act on it today, but clearly, she was going to need a little push.

"I-I—What do you mean?" Lucy forced out a laugh. "I don't want you, I...I don't want you!" she repeated as if that would somehow make it more convincing.

Sherry turned to lie on her back, propping herself up on her elbows, completely unbothered by the fact that she was left uncovered as the towel fell to her side. "Oh?" She quirked a perfectly arched brow as she tilted her head, a small pout forming on her lips. "You don't want me?"

"I—Well," Lucy let out another awkward laugh as she tried to figure out what to say. "That's not... Well, it's not like—"

"I want you," Sherry admitted easily, smiling when Lucy's eyes nearly bulged out of her head. "I want you to touch me. To kiss me. Make me feel good...And I want to do the same for you. You don't want that?"

Lucy was stunned into silence. Why wouldn't she? This was literally one of her wet dreams come to life! How many times had she sat around, daydreaming about what it would be like to have Sherry say those exact words to her? And now it was actually happening? Lucy wondered if she was just hallucinating.

Sherry giggled at the dumbstruck look on Lucy's face before yanking on the girl's shirt to pull her closer, and Lucy gasped as she was suddenly hovering over Sherry, their breasts rubbing together, only separated by the fabric of Lucy's crop top.

Sherry tugged at the hem of it as she stared into Lucy's pretty, round eyes. "Take this off."

Lucy had never followed orders so quickly before in her entire life. She pulled the shirt over her head, exposing her bare breasts, and she tried not to feel self-conscious as Sherry stared at her unabashedly.

"They're–smaller than yours," Lucy stuttered out in an attempt to point out her insecurity before Sherry could, but she only ended up feeling even more stupid for pointing out the obvious. "Sorry. I mean, not for the size of my boobs. I mean–"

"I like them," Sherry giggled and licked her lip as she brought a hand up to grope Lucy's breast. Lucy's breath hitched as her body tensed up, a shiver traveling down her spine. Sherry grinned, staring up at her with half-lidded eyes. "So cute. Are you a virgin?"

"What? No." Lucy blushed. "I've been with

another girl before..." Although it was a long time ago, and Lucy had barely managed to cum.

"Mm," Sherry hummed before sitting up. Lucy gasped as Sherry maneuvered them with ease, and suddenly, Lucy was the one on her back, staring up at Sherry as Sherry hovered over her. "Mind if I take these off?" Sherry asked, and it took a few moments for the words to register, but Lucy quickly nodded when she realized that Sherry was tugging at her shorts.

"Yeah–No? No, I don't mind!"

The giggle that Sherry let out as she tugged down Lucy's shorts didn't make it any easier for Lucy to fight off her permanent blush. That, Lucy realized, was the fond little giggle that Sherry let out every time Lucy did something that she thought was cute. And the thought of Sherry finding her cute had Lucy's stomach knotting up, butterflies fluttering all around inside it.

"Wow." Sherry's sultry voice pulled Lucy out of her lovestruck thoughts and back into the moment. "No bra and no panties? Someone came prepared." She smirked. "Did you, by any chance, plan this?"

"No!" Lucy shook her head. She never in a million years could have anticipated that this would be happening, but she sure was glad that she'd chosen to wear the bare minimum anyway.

"Oh? So then you're just a little slut who likes to walk around with no underwear on?" Sherry smirked, an amused gleam in her eye as Lucy's widened. Lucy had to fight back an audible moan and the urge to beg Sherry to call her a slut again. Instead, she simply nodded, trying to keep her cool.

"Yeah, I guess I am. But let's not forget what you showed up wearing."

Nothing but a thin, silk robe that Lucy couldn't believe she felt comfortable leaving the house in.

Sherry let out a surprised laugh at Lucy's teasing. "Well, well, well. Look who finally grew some balls. What, are you done behaving like a shy little schoolgirl with a big, fat crush?"

Lucy crinkled her nose. "Don't bring up balls when we're about to have sex. Are you trying to ruin the mood?"

Sherry rolled her eyes and let out a giggle before leaning down to give Lucy a kiss. It was a quick peck, at first, but Lucy surprised her yet again by pulling her down and taking her mouth in a long and heated kiss.

Lucy licked Sherry's bottom lip before pushing her tongue between the girl's plump, pink lips, and

Sherry opened up easily, groaning when Lucy's tongue slid over hers. Sherry tilted her head to deepen the kiss and tangled her tongue with Lucy's, letting out a squeak of surprise when Lucy pulled away and bit down on her bottom lip before sucking on it gently.

The two of them became lost in the sloppy kiss, growing increasingly desperate the longer it continued. Lucy moaned into Sherry's mouth as Sherry began playing with her breasts, pinching one of her nipples while gently rubbing a thumb over the other. Meanwhile, Lucy's hands were roaming Sherry's body, sliding over each and every one of her curves, digging into her soft skin.

Sherry pulled away from their kiss and began pressing open-mouthed kisses along Lucy's jawline, all over Lucy's neck, and down to her breasts, where Sherry placed all her focus.

"Shit," Lucy murmured, lazily running her fingers through Sherry's hair as Sherry sucked one of her nipples into her mouth. "I'm sensitive t-there," she moaned, squirming as she squeezed her eyes shut.

"I bet you're sensitive here too," Sherry commented before pushing two fingers between the folds of Lucy's cunt. Lucy gasped as Sherry slid her fingers up and down her center a few times before rubbing them over her clit.

Sherry leaned up to kiss Lucy again as she gave the girl's clit a pinch that had her flinching and letting out a breathy moan. When Sherry's fingers traveled down, the tips of them poking at Lucy's entrance, Lucy quickly pulled away from their kiss again.

"I can't–I won't last long if you…"

"Isn't that the whole point?" Sherry smirked. "I want to make you cum all over my fingers."

Before Lucy could say anything, Sherry leaned down to give her another extended kiss before pulling away and repositioning herself again. She turned her back to Lucy before straddling her stomach, then wiggled her hips as she looked back at Lucy. "I want you to eat me out. Okay?"

"Fuck, yes," Lucy groaned as she grabbed Sherry's sides, pulling her back a little. She didn't waste any time before pushing Sherry's cheeks apart and pushing her tongue between the lips of the girl's cunt.

Sherry sucked in a sharp breath as Lucy's tongue began exploring her pussy, flicking over her clit a few times before swirling around her entrance and then poking inside of it. Sherry just about melted into a puddle right then and there, her arms giving out on her as she pressed her torso against Lucy's stomach.

It took a couple of seconds for her to pull herself together enough to focus on making Lucy feel good too, but when she finally did, she spread the lips of Lucy's cunt apart with two fingers, immediately swirling her tongue around the girl's clit before beginning to suck on it. She slowly pushed her middle finger inside of Lucy's hole, groaning as she felt the way Lucy twitched and spasmed around her.

Sherry replaced her one finger with two and started up a steady pace, thrusting them in and out of Lucy's cunt quickly as she allowed her spit to dribble off her tongue and between Lucy's folds. Lucy was already dripping wet with her own slick, the wet sound of Sherry's fingers plunging in and out of her filling the room along with their moans.

Sherry used her other hand to hold Lucy's hips down as they bucked up, the girl's thighs quivering as she pushed herself against Sherry's fingers, meeting her thrusts. Sherry could tell that she was already getting close by the way her moans were getting louder and her tongue moved irregularly, losing its rhythm.

Still, Sherry could barely keep herself together as Lucy's tongue worked its magic. Lucy lapped Sherry's wetness up greedily, nibbling on the sensitive skin around her cunt, spitting into Sherry's hole before slurping the mess right back out. She had to keep her arms wrapped around Sherry's thighs to keep the girl from running away from the intense pleasure, and she was determined to make Sherry cum on her tongue. She wanted to taste even more of her, and she could tell that she was getting closer.

"Fuck," Sherry slurred, pushing herself back against Lucy's tongue as she began rubbing quick circles around Lucy's clit. Lucy gasped, the pit of her stomach burning hot with pleasure that was threatening to spill over at any moment. "Yes, just like that, baby. Feels so good–just like that!" Sherry's eyes rolled into the back of her head as she continued fucking herself back onto Lucy's tongue, biting her lip to keep herself from getting too loud. Not that it helped much. When Lucy began sucking on her clit again, her whole body tensed up before suddenly, waves of pleasure were crashing over her, and her orgasm was bursting out of her. She came with a loud shout, gasping for breath as Lucy held her in place and continued eating her out even as the pleasure started to become overwhelming.

Lucy wasn't far behind. Sherry could feel the girl clenching and unclenching around her fingers as she continued pounding into her, crooking her fingers until they hit the small bundle of nerves inside of her. Lucy let out a string of curses and loud moans of her own as her back arched off the bed and her legs snapped shut, only for Sherry to push them apart once again before continuing to finger her.

Lucy was seeing stars, and Sherry was seeing nothing but blur as the two of them fucked each other through their orgasms. They were both nothing more than a pile of sweaty skin and bones that felt more like jelly as they tried to come down from their high. Sherry managed to roll off of Lucy and reposition herself so that she was lying beside her. Lucy let out some sort of tired noise—a mix of a delighted laugh, a tired groan, and a satisfied moan—as she rolled over until she was lying half on top of Sherry and half on the bed.

Sherry grunted as Lucy kneed her in the side while attempting to wrap a leg around her, but aside from that, neither of them said or did anything aside from trying to catch their breath.

Until a few minutes later, when Lucy was mostly conscious of the world around her again and had enough strength to lift her head and look at Sherry.

"Well, that was fucking amazing!" She paused

for a few moments before sending Sherry a hopeful look. "We're gonna have a round two, right?"

A lazy grin made its way onto Sherry's face as she attempted to nod, but she was still too tired to do such a strenuous activity. It had been a long time since she'd cum that hard. Still, there was only one right answer to the question.

"Obviously."

# He Likes To Watch
## By Victoria Jimenez

"Come on in." Carmen smiled as she opened the front door to let Carlos in. "I'm glad you're here! I've been horny all day, and it's about time someone did something about it..." Her dark eyes trailed over to look at the man sitting on the living room couch, and her gaze turned cold as she let out a quiet sigh. "Just ignore my husband, Ray. He's not man enough for me, so you're going to fuck me while he watches. Maybe he'll pick up some tips."

The man all but whined as Carlos chuckled and looked him up and down before turning to Carmen again. "No problem. Do you want it on the couch, or would you prefer it if I fucked you right in the middle of you and your husband's bed?"

Carmen bit her lip and pressed her thighs

together as she stared up at the smug-looking man. She could hardly stand to wait any longer, and honestly, she didn't care if he decided to take her right in the middle of the living room floor, on the couch, against the wall, whatever—but then again, her getting fucked by another man in their bed would be far more humiliating for Ray.

So with a large smirk on her face, she wordlessly grabbed Carlos' hand and turned to lead him toward the bedroom. She didn't even need to look in order to know that Ray was scurrying behind them like a lost puppy. He just barely managed to make it into the room before they slammed the door shut in his face.

"Okay, let's get straight to it. I want it doggy style," Carmen said as she unhooked her bra and shimmied out of her underwear before climbing onto the bed. "Ray can never last for more than a minute when we do doggy style." She rolled her eyes.

"I'm not surprised," Carlos murmured as he positioned himself behind Carmen, grabbing her hips to pull her toward him and pushing her down until her back was arched. She looked picture perfect in this position.

Carlos took a few moments to explore her body, tugging at the long, dark brown hair that cascaded down her back, running his hands along her smooth, golden skin, and kneading the meaty flesh of her large behind between his fingertips. He sucked in a breath when he pushed her cheeks apart to get a better look at her cunt and saw that she was already dripping wet.

"A man like that can't handle a woman like you," he continued as he allowed his middle finger to run between her folds. Carmen shivered, twitching a little as he briefly poked the tip of his finger inside her hole before pulling it away again. "How did he even manage to convince you to settle for him?"

"I thought he was a real man," she grumbled under her breath. "He was handsome, tall, strong-looking, all muscles. He had a voice so deep that it made me want to drop my panties right on the spot—and most of all, he had the biggest cock that I'd ever seen in my life..." She sighed and shook her head as she turned to look at him.

Unsurprisingly, Ray was in the midst of slowly stroking himself, already a little red in the face, chest already heaving as his dark eyes watched the two of them closely. He bit down on his plump lower lip, thumb sliding over the slit of his cock. He didn't even pretend to not be turned on by the sight of his own wife on all fours for some other man.

Carmen rolled her eyes. "It's such a damn

shame. Such a waste for him to be gifted with such an impressive cock when he doesn't even know how to use the damn thing properly!" she scoffed, and Ray let out a low noise, something along the lines of a whine or a whimper, or some other unmanly sound that caused her to roll her eyes again before turning to face away from him. "He's so pathetic, I swear... Carlos, why don't you go ahead and show him how a real man does it, hm? I don't need any prep. Just get inside me!"

Carlos was unfazed by her orders, simply grabbing the back of her neck and shoving her face into the pillows once she'd turned to glare at him after a few seconds had gone by without him doing what she'd told him to.

"Well, for starters, a real man doesn't take orders from mouthy little brats with bad attitudes like you," he chuckled. "Believe me, I'll fuck you when I'm good and ready. Just be quiet and stay still for me until then, hm?" he mocked.

Carmen lifted her head, turning to send him another glare, but she didn't open her mouth to say anything else, so he ignored it, smirking as he plunged two fingers inside of her, crooking them for a moment before pulling them out. The hard look melted off of Carmen's face in an instant, her eyes widening a little and her lips parting as she sucked in a quiet breath.

"So wet," he commented, pausing for a moment to suck on the two fingers that had just been inside her. He let out a satisfied hum before pulling them out of his mouth and burying them inside of her cunt again. "You really weren't lying about being horny all day, huh?"

Carmen was a little too preoccupied with rocking herself back against his fingers to answer. Two fingers really weren't enough to clench her craving–she'd been fantasizing about being filled to the brim with cock all day, just dying to finally experience the wonderful feeling of being stretched and full again–but it was something, which was better than nothing. She could feel the tips of his fingers just barely grazing the soft spot inside of her every time she pushed herself back, and she closed her eyes, her brows furrowing as she put all of her focus on that feeling.

"And you have the audacity to call your husband pathetic," Carlos snickered. "You're the one acting like a bitch in heat."

"Maybe I wouldn't be so desperate if my good-for-nothing husband took care of my needs!" she spat, her accent becoming thicker as her words slurred together. Carlos glanced over at Ray, scoffing as he caught sight of the man pouting with his hand wrapped around his cock.

"Can't argue with that." He narrowed his eyes at Ray before turning to look at Carmen again. She let out a loud whine when he removed his fingers, and then a surprised squeal when he pinched her clit harshly between his thumb and forefinger. "You want me to fuck you, Carmen?"

"Isn't that what I've been telling you this whole time?!" she growled.

"Yes, but you haven't asked. Ask me to fuck you. Beg me to fuck you."

"I've never had to beg a man for anything in my whole life, especially not to fuck me."

"There's a first time for everything."

"I'm not going to beg you–"

"That's fine. I can just go back home and call up some other desperate slut who'll be just as eager for me to fuck her, and you can stay here with your pathetic excuse for a husband and enjoy the fifteen seconds of sex that he'll be able to give you before he blows his load and calls it a night. Your choice."

Carmen stared at Carlos with the most venomous expression that she could muster up, and Carlos simply quirked a brow at her, his lips pulling up into his usual smirk as he moved to get off the bed only to have her reach back to grab his wrist.

"Please," she gritted out. "Fuck me."

"You can do better than that, sweetheart. Where's your enthusiasm?"

"Carlos—" She heaved a heavy sigh as she sent him her best set of puppy dog eyes. A stark contrast to her previous death glare. "I want it more than anything. I want you to fuck me, okay? Please? Will you please fuck me?"

"Good job asking for what you want." He smiled. "Now beg like I told you to."

"That was me begging!" she whined, slapping the mattress in frustration as if that would do anything aside from making the smug expression on Carlos' face become even more unbearable.

"Not quite. Try it again. Or you can let Ray–"

"Please just fuck me already!" she cried. "I just want to feel full and–and I want you to fuck me until I can't even think anymore, and I want you to show Ray what it looks like to pleasure a woman properly, and I want to cum! I want you to make me cum, and I want you to cum inside me too and–"

"No!" Ray suddenly called from the couch, eyes as wide as saucers as the two of them turned to look at him. Carlos rolled his eyes at the man before letting out a cruel laugh.

"What's the matter, Ray? You don't want another man coming inside your wife?"

"No..." he practically whispered as he stared between the two of them.

"Maybe you should have thought about that before she called me over." Carlos shrugged. Ray watched with a helpless expression on his face as Carlos grabbed Carmen's sides, pushing her down until her back was arched even more, her ass lifted high up in the air, ready and waiting.

He wrapped a hand around the base of his cock, rubbing the tip of it between Carmen's folds a few times before sinking inside of her with one swift thrust. Carmen gasped and choked on her own spit as she was caught off guard. One second she'd been clenching around nothing, wiggling her ass in the air as she waited for an intrusion that she was starting to think would never come, and the next, Carlos' balls were slapping against her cunt as he breached her, his cock resting hard and heavy inside of her, dragging against her inner walls as he pulled out before slamming back in again.

Carlos gave a couple of hard thrusts just to hear the sound of his skin slapping against hers as she let out strained cries, moans of pleasure mixed with whimpers of pain and words of thanks slurred together as she finally got what she wanted from him.

It was only a couple of seconds later when he picked up the pace and stuck to a steady rhythm, beginning to pound into her with harsh thrusts that caused the whole bed to rock, the headboard crashing into the wall and Carmen clinging to the sheets in an attempt to keep herself steady.

"There we go." Carlos let out a breathless chuckle, his eyes glued to Carmen's ass as it smacked against his hips repeatedly. "You're finally getting what you wanted, now what should you say?"

"Tha–Thank y-you," she stammered, sucking in a sharp breath when Carlos grabbed her hair, winding it around his fist for a better grip as he forced her upper body up off the bed. He turned her head until she was facing Ray, and she couldn't help but moan as she caught sight of him frowning with his hand wrapped around the base of his angry-red cock, clearly trying to keep himself from coming prematurely.

"Jesus." She let out a breathy laugh, trying to keep her eyes on him even as they threatened to slip shut. "I've never seen a sadder sight in my entire life. How could you be sitting there playing with your big, dumb, useless cock while another man takes care of your wife in your own bed? Don't you have any f-fucking shame?"

She paused and bit her lip, trying to find the strength to speak again, but it took her a while to find her voice as Carlos tugged harder on her hair, slapping her ass with his free hand before pushing down on her lower back again. She was starting to see stars dancing around in her vision as he split her open on his cock, her cunt throbbing and pulsating enough to distract her from berating her husband for a short time.

Everything faded away for a moment as she melted into the mattress, focusing on nothing aside from the feeling of the big, strong man on top of her forcing his cock in and out of her at a rapid speed. By the time she remembered what she was supposed to be doing–throwing insults at her spineless husband–she was drooling.

Even drooling and stuttering and shaking like a leaf as Carlos drew his hand back and spanked her several more times until his handprint was visible on her skin, she was still somehow less pitiful than Ray.

"H-How does it feel to–ah–" She sucked in a sharp breath as Carlos changed his position slightly, angling his hips in order to fuck her even deeper.

Now he was slamming right into her G-spot with every thrust, and Carmen could feel her pussy twitching and her skin heating up and stomach tingling as she got closer to her orgasm. "—to see a real man fucking your w-wife and doing what you never could?" she finished, giggling as she watched Ray's expression morph into one of a kicked puppy.

"You think you sitting there looking sad is going to make me feel bad for you? No, I feel bad for me. This is how I deserve to be fucked all the time, but instead, I have to put up with you and your deplorable little cock! You're so fucking hopeless, Ray, I swear! So pointless for you to have such a nice cock and no skills to use it–Shit!" she gasped when Carlos let go of her hair, her face suddenly buried in the sheets beneath her. She tried to lift her head, but Carlos' hand was pressed against the back of it, effectively holding her down.

"Sorry, sweetheart, nothing personal. It's just that I'm never gonna be able to cum if I have to keep listening to you go on and on about your husband's so-called 'cock,'" he grunted. "I'll let you sit up again if you can keep that big mouth of yours shut, though. Think you can do that?"

She groaned a short slew of indecipherable words, and Carlos took that as a yes, grabbing her hair and lifting her head again before pulling her in for a rough kiss. The angle was awkward, uncomfortable, and borderline painful for Carmen, who had to strain her neck in order to meet his lips, but that and the way Carlos grabbed her breast with his other hand before sliding it down to clutch her stomach only added to her pleasure. She felt dirty and thoroughly used, and there was no better feeling on Earth, in her opinion.

"You fuck me so good," she moaned once he pulled away from her lips. "So good, Papi, so good, so good–"

"Shit," Carlos groaned as he felt her pussy spasming around his cock, slipping out of her for a moment as her wetness made things a little more slippery, but he quickly pushed himself inside of her again, drilling into her with newfound determination as he chased his own orgasm.

Carmen screamed as he slammed in and out of her repeatedly, holding her down and making her take the brutal pounding even as she tried to squirm away from the overwhelming feeling of pleasure. Eventually, she gave up, her body becoming pliant underneath his as her mind drifted off to God knew where. She was barely conscious as she drooled and cried and screamed and moaned until her vocal cords were sore. She couldn't make out the filthy words that Carlos was murmuring in her ear, barely even registered him wrapping his hand around her neck and squeezing until she struggled to take a full breath. But the unmistakable feeling of him pulling out of her brought her back to reality with a sudden jolt.

She whined, squirming around just slightly, wiggling her ass as if to entice him to fill her up with his cock again, but it didn't work. Carlos groaned, throwing his head back as he stroked himself quickly. Despite what he'd said earlier, he knew that coming inside of her wasn't an option, but covering her plump ass with his seed instead was just fine with him.

All it took was him looking down between them and catching sight of her sopping wet cunt, thoroughly fucked open and still convulsing as her wetness leaked out of her and onto the sheets, and suddenly, he was shooting his load all over her ass with a low groan.

Carmen let out a quiet moan as she felt his cum landing over the globes of her ass, some dripping onto her pussy, between her lips, making her feel even filthier than she already had before. Her cunt throbbed as she turned and watched Carlos wordlessly climb off the bed and head to the bathroom once he was finished. It was as if he'd gotten what he'd wanted and now he was done with her. The thought made her feel low, used, and horny all over again as a result, but she ignored the heartbeat between her legs and let out a soft moan as she turned over to lie on her back instead, then turned her head to look at Ray, who was already standing up and walking over.

He wordlessly climbed on top of her, stroking his cock as he stared down at her heaving chest, her big breasts on full display and looking just as perfect as they always did. He groaned as he came all over her tits, his cum splattering over her nipples and the soft flesh of her breasts until he had no more of his seed left to give.

By the time he was finished, he was breathless and trembling from the intensity of his orgasm, struggling to hold himself upright as he threw his head back.

"Fuck," he murmured when he'd finally managed to breathe again. "Thank you, baby."

"You're welcome," Carmen giggled, suddenly sounding like her usual, shy self. "Happy birthday!"

"Happy birthday to me," Ray chuckled before leaning down to press a gentle kiss to her lips.

# Mistress
## My Amanda Moss

The bed beside Richard was cold when he woke, and in his sleepy state, he glanced around for his wife. There was no sight of her in the room, and he experienced a sudden jolt of excitement when he tried to move his hands. They were each tied to a bedpost, he realized, and he was completely naked.

He heard footsteps coming up the hallway stairs. Seconds later, his bedroom door swung open, and Tara stood in the doorway. Just the sight of her took his breath away, as it always did. She wore a black leather corset that covered her torso and pushed her breasts up so they were almost spilling over, and her pussy was completely exposed. Black boots were laced up to her knees, with a sexy heel that clicked with every step.

Richard loved his wife. She was a spectacular woman, and she was the perfect housewife. He never had to request anything from her; it was almost as if she could read his mind. The two of them flowed together flawlessly, and he couldn't imagine being with anyone else.

Richard worked long hours during the week as the CEO of a large investment company. Every day, he managed hundreds of people and their duties, and it was tiresome. He had every weekend off, and to take a break from his normal routine, he let Tara take control of him and boss him around. It was quite fun.

His wife, though innocent during the week, was quite the dominatrix. During the weekends, she was his Mistress, and she made damn sure he knew it.

She tilted her head to the side, glancing him over with a disapproving look. "Do you think you can just lie around all day?" she crooned, slowly strutting toward him. His eyes followed her as she approached his side of the bed, swinging her leg over and straddling his lap. *God, she's so sexy*, he thought, admiring her body as she stared down at him. *I'm one lucky man.* "Don't you know that there's work to be done?" She gave him a sharp slap across his face, and he did his best not to wince. "I asked you a question, Richard."

"Yes, Mistress, I know there's work to be done," he responded quickly, more awake after the slap. She was the dominatrix, he was her submissive; in his half-asleep state, that hadn't fully registered.

He gazed up at her as she shifted her body forward so that she hovered over his face. He had the perfect view of her beautiful, juicy pussy. "Are you ready to get to work?" she demanded.

"I'm ready, Mistress." He could taste her already and was ready to do her bidding.

Tara straddled his face, moving her pussy dangerously close to his mouth. His mouth began to water for her. "I bet you are. Now get started."

She lowered herself onto his face, applying force, and he was greeted with the familiar feeling of her wet pussy and tight ass against his face and tongue.

His tongue mixed back and forth around her clit, and she sighed. "Oh, you're so good. You're such a good boy. Lick my clit harder." He did as she commanded, rewarded with a soft moan. "Good boy. Move your tongue in circles."

He lapped up every drop of her sweet nectar, inhaling her intoxicating scent. Anything for his Mistress. Her breathing was coming faster and faster, and he longed to be able to touch her with his hands. He itched to run his fingers along her breasts, to tease and pluck at her nipples until she screamed, but today she was in control.

"Harder, harder!" she demanded, crying out. Her entire body spasmed above him, so hard he could feel the trembling in her pussy. "Don't stop!" She rode his face for a few more moments before lightly lifting himself up, freeing his lips.

She steadied herself against the wall for a moment, breathing heavily, before staring down at Richard once more. She leaned down, her hair brushing his face and tickling. He shivered at the sensation, eager to please her more.

Tara whispered in his ear. "That was... mmm, so good." A shiver wracked his whole body as her breath tingled against his skin, and his cock rose just a little more. "You're such a good boy." She laughed as she pulled his head up by his hair, gripping tightly. "Tell me how good of a boy you are."

"I'm a good boy, Mistress," he responded rapidly, desperate for more abuse. He loved it just as much as she did.

She opened her legs once again, and as she reached down to rub her clit, she took him by surprise and started rubbing herself on his face. He groaned with pleasure as his mouth was suddenly filled with her pussy once more. He continued to lick and suck at her delicate pussy lips; he couldn't get enough.

"Eat me out until I cum," she told him, and he was more than willing. "Tell me what you're going to do."

"I'm going to eat you out until you cum," he mumbled through her pussy lips, tongue-fucking her.

He had never felt so hungry for her before, he was desperate to please her. His lips and tongue were burning with her taste, so delicious. He sucked and licked her pussy, flicking his tongue back and forth across her clit.

Her fingers gripped the back of his head, her thighs squeezing his head tightly as she panted above him.

His cock was hard and pressing against his underwear. His balls felt swollen, and they ached with the need to release, but only with her permission. He could only hope she would give it to him soon.

Tara began to moan. Her moans came faster and faster until she was breathing in short, ragged breaths. His tongue was growing sore moving back and forth inside her pussy, but he was determined to do as she demanded.

Her hips bucked against his head as she came

hard, gasping. "Oh fuck, oh fuck," she moaned. "God, you have suck a talented fucking mouth."

He kissed the inside of her thighs as she caught her breath again, loving the feel of her soft skin. "Kissing me is not going to bring you better treatment," Tara told him. She slid off his body and leaned over him, undoing the binding around his wrists. "Stand up," she commanded, stepping back. He hurried to do as she told him, and she beckoned for him to follow him with her finger. He followed closely behind her, keeping his eyes on her sweet, exposed ass.

She led him into their spare bedroom, shoving him inside and slamming the door shut behind them. It was a room they only used on the weekends, when Tara was having her way. It was their BDSM dungeon; within, they had muzzles, rope, collars, wrist and ankle restraints, and a large, soft bed fitted with velvet sheets. Just the sight of it made his cock rise all the way up, and he curiously wondered what his Mistress was going to do to him today.

"Get on the bed," she ordered him, smacking his ass to get him to move faster. As he climbed on, she shoved him again so that he was on his back. Above him, suspended from the ceiling, was a spreader bar. It hadn't been there the previous weekend, so she must have just purchased it. Tara did love her toys, and she had a credit card solely for the purpose of her purchasing whatever she wanted.

"Lift your legs up." He did so, watching excitedly as his wife secured his ankles to either side of the spreader bar. He was utterly exposed, and the thought of it made it the hairs on his arm stand on end. She turned away from him for only a moment, grinning wickedly when she returned and presented two pairs of handcuffs. "Hold out your hands."

He winced as she tightly secured each of his hands to different bedposts, gulping with anticipation as she dragged her hand down his chest. He was so hard, his erection glaringly obvious, and she laughed at him. "I'm sorry, is this making you horny?" she teased, slapping his cock lightly with the palm of her hand. The feel of her skin on his delicate member only intensified his desire for her.

"Yes, Mistress. You make me horny," he told her honestly.

"Flattery will get you nowhere. You're not allowed to cum yet, Richard. Not until I've had my way." She walked over to the wall, exaggerating the sway of her hips, and paused in front of her sizable collection of cock rings. "My, my, my. Which one should we play with?" She delicately dragged her hand along each one, glancing over at Richard with a sly look. "Why don't you choose?"

Somehow, he knew this was a trick. No matter which cock ring he chose, she was going to select the one she wanted to use. She likely already had one in mind. His eyes scanned over them, landing on a simple one. It was fitted with loops so that its size could be adjusted. "That one, Mistress," he stated, nodding his head toward it.

She followed his gaze and laughed. "You would choose that one, wouldn't you? You're a pussy, Richard. I want to hear you say it."

"I'm a pussy, Mistress," he said obediently.

"No, I have something a little more... adventurous in mind." She reached for the highest one on the wall, and his gaze once more went to her delicious ass.

The ring she chose had a connecting chain with clamps connected to it, which were meant for his nipples. She walked over to him and slowly, delicately, slid the ring onto him. She lightly traced her index finger up and down his shaft, gauging his reaction as she deliberately licked her full lips. "My, you're quite large. Do you want me?"

"Yes, Mistress." He wanted her so fucking badly

that his body was trembling. He craved more of her touch.

"Do you want to fuck me?"

"Yes, Mistress."

"Louder!" she shouted, grabbing hold of his cock and squeezing. His body jerked at the sudden pressure, and the touch alone almost made him cum.

"Yes, Mistress!" he screamed.

"That's too bad, because that's not what's going to happen next." He winced as she connected each clamp to one of his nipples, making sure they were secured tightly.

His heartbeat picked up when she grabbed hold of her flogger, lightly twirling it around. Out of her paddles and whips, she enjoyed using the flogger the most, and Richard enjoyed it as well. It brought him both pain and pleasure. "Because you've been naughty, haven't you?"

"Yes, Mistress," he breathed.

She stood before him, holding the flogger in her right hand. Gently, she dragged it along his cock, and his eyes almost rolled into the back of his head at how amazing the leather felt on his skin. "Say it louder."

"Yes, Mistress."

He gasped when she stepped back and smacked his bare ass with the flogger. It stung, and one of the strands clipped the edge of his ball sack. She shook her head in disappointment, clicking her tongue. "Dear me, it seems I didn't do it hard enough. You barely made any noise."

She flogged him again, and he grunted with pain. "Did I hit you hard enough, Richard?"

"Yes, Mistress."

She hit him harder, and he cried out as his lust grew. "I think you're lying, Richard. Am I hitting you hard enough, Richard?"

"No, Mistress."

"Should I hit you harder then?"

"Yes, Mistress." *Fuck yes.*

She swatted him again and again, each time harder than the last. "Will you lie to me again?"

"No, Mistress," he whimpered. Richard grunted with both pain and pleasure as his wife spanked him once more. He loved for her to take control. She lifted her arms, giving him freedom to lift his backside high, ready for her to strike again and proving his eagerness. She grinned unexpectedly but tried to hide it. He sighed, moaning as his wife's palm connected with his cheek instead of the flogger.

"God, you're so hard," she commented, amused. She swiped his tip with her finger, gazing down curiously at the droplet of cum on her finger. Slowly, she licked it off, and more of his juices leaked out in response. "You want to cum, don't you?"

"Yes, Mistress," he all but begged.

"Oh, I know you do. Don't worry, it's almost time." Her smile was mischievous as she pulled a metal wand from behind her back. He wanted to frown. He hadn't noticed her grab it, but he should have known; it was one of her favorite toys.

He moaned as she slipped the wand into his ass, jumping at how cold it was and internally amazed at how easily it entered him. It was ribbed, and he felt each rib as it entered his anal cavity. She slid it slowly in and out, and he felt his cock throb at the stimulation. "Do you like that?" she whispered, crouching down so that he could no longer see her. Her breath tickled his crotch. "Do you like feeling like there's a cock in your ass?"

"Yes, Mistress!"

It was unnerving, having her mouth that close to his crotch. He was desperate for release; his cock was throbbing so hard it was almost painful. She slid the wand farther in, chuckling lightly.

"I think you've been punished enough, you bad boy. You took it well." She lowered her voice. "Do you think you deserve a reward?"

"Yes!" he moaned as she began to lightly stroke his shaft.

She tightened her grip on him. "Yes what?"

"Yes, Mistress!"

*Oh, God.* She continued to run her hand up and down his cock, and he was well aware of how much she was enjoying herself. "Do you think you deserve to have my mouth on your cock?"

"Yes! Yes, Mistress!"

Richard lifted his head, watching his wife with amazement as she took his penis into her mouth and began to suck on it, her hands lovingly fondling his balls. She loved to play with his balls, but she had never given him such intimate attention while she was in dominatrix mode. Richard couldn't take his eyes off her as she played with him. He could feel himself about to climax any second, and he didn't want to miss a moment, though he tried to hold it in.

"No cumming until I say so," Tara warned him, her hands replacing her mouth on his genitals. "It's not time."

"I..."—Richard stopped to gasp for air—"...can't...hold...on...Mistress..." He felt himself going, a flood of pleasure threatening to overwhelm him. It wasn't enough to push him over, but it was close.

"No cumming, or I swear I will spank the shit out of you!"

With that, Tara continued sucking him to the edge and held him there. He could feel himself slipping away. He couldn't hold back his desire anymore. As her hands rubbed his cock, he felt himself tingle in her hands. As he envisioned her bouncing up and down on his cock, moaning, he felt another rush of lust and desire. He was about to burst; it was too intense.

"Richard, don't you dare come until I say so!" She licked up his shaft, licking his balls before wrapping her tongue around the tip.

"Oh fuck," he sighed, shifting his hips. "Please fuck me, Mistress."

"You want me to fuck you?" She smiled. "No need to beg me, darling." She began to suck him harder and faster, squeezing his cock in her mouth and licking him. She wanted his pleasure.

"Please fuck me, just like this. I want to feel my cock fill your pussy with cum, Mistress," he begged her.

She took his shaft and began stroking again. "Is that what you want? To fill me with your cum?" she asked, amused.

"Yes, please fuck me. Please don't stop." His balls

tightened, and his cock twitched, pleading for more of her attention.

In seconds, her outfit was off, thrown to the floor. Her perky breasts exposed, she straddled him, slipping his cock deep inside of her. He was delighted to feel how wet she was. She let out a soft moan as she settled herself. "The same rules apply," she said almost breathlessly. "You are not allowed to cum until I say so."

"Fuck, fuck," he cried as he clenched his legs in pleasure, her pussy gripping his cock. "Please Mistress, make me come," he pleaded as she rocked her hips.

"You cannot have your orgasm until I say it's time." She continued riding him, letting his cock sink into her pussy.

He knew if he came, he would be in big trouble, and she would punish him harshly. He loved the way his cock felt in her pussy, and he loved her to ride him, but he wasn't sure how much longer he could hold his orgasm in. She was going to do what she wanted until she was satisfied.

He loved the way she rode his cock. She leaned forward a bit, sliding her pussy down the length of him and winking. Her pussy was clenched so tightly around him that he almost came. He was having a hard time controlling himself. This was the most intense feeling of pure pleasure he had ever experienced.

She leaned forward again, and this time she was aiming her pussy downward as she rode him. She was riding him and squeezing him and fucking him with her pussy. He wished he could grip on to her hips or the headboard to steady himself, but the handcuffs held his hands firmly in place. She was bouncing on his cock faster and faster.

Tara began bucking and rubbing her pussy on him with force, her gasps coming faster and faster until she spasmed above him. The spasms in her pussy threw him overboard, and he screamed with her as white-hot pleasure shot through him, overwhelming his senses.

She shuddered again, relaxing down onto his cock and giving him a satisfied smile, her cheeks flushed. "I didn't tell you to cum, but you're forgiven. Good boy."

# Who's The Boss
By Jordan W. Miller

Rob tapped his foot impatiently as he knocked on the door more times than what was necessary, until finally, he heard an annoyed shout. "Come in!"

He flung the door open and slammed it shut behind him, taking long strides over to the surprised-looking woman's desk until he was standing right in front of it, staring her down.

"Rob, what are you still doing here? It's 5 p.m. You were supposed to get off an hour ago, weren't you?"

"I'm here to turn in my letter of resignation," he told her before thrusting the paper onto her desk. "I no longer wish to work here."

The dark-skinned woman's brown eyes widened even more as she quickly skimmed the paper before looking up at him again. She shook her head, shooting out of her seat and practically running to the other side of her desk to stand in front of him.

"What? But this is so sudden! You're one of this company's best employees! You've been working here for the last four and a half years, and you were next in line for a huge promotion! You can't just up and quit like this—"

"Tracey, I don't give a damn about any of that, and you know I don't." Rob sent her a hard look as he took a step closer to her. "While I work here, you're my boss, and I'm your employee, and it's against company policy for us to have any sort of relationship outside of a strictly professional one. You know that."

"Yes, but—"

"So I quit," Rob cut her off. "I can find another stuffy office job anywhere, and a man with my credentials will have no problem finding work with some other hotshot company. But where the hell am I supposed to find another woman like you?"

"I..." Tracey let out an exasperated laugh, shaking her head at him. "This is...Really, are you sure you don't want to think about this a little more? Quitting your job just for the sake of being with me is crazy!"

"No, it's not," Rob chuckled. "Missing out on the opportunity to be with the woman I love because of some silly job is crazy. I need you way more than I need this job, do you understand?"

Tracey opened her mouth in an attempt to say something else, but nothing came out. It wasn't very often that she was left speechless, but Rob always seemed to be the cause when she was.

Rob took a few more moments to search Tracey's chocolate eyes, trying to gauge her reaction. It was clear that she was surprised, but he wasn't quite sure why. He would jump into the middle of ongoing traffic or fling himself off a bridge for her without a second thought if she asked him to, and he thought that much was obvious.

But maybe not. Maybe he hadn't made it clear how much he truly loved her. He'd never been good with words, and expressing his feelings freely was a foreign concept to him, but he could show her how he felt about her better than he could tell her.

He pulled her in for a heated kiss before he could even think to stop himself, groaning as she immediately reciprocated it. Tracey tilted her head to deepen the kiss, wrapping her arms around Rob's neck as he pressed the palm of his hand against her lower back to pull her closer, his other hand squeezing her hip as he maneuvered them until Tracey's back was to her desk.

He easily lifted her up, setting her on the desk and standing between her legs as he haphazardly moved things around to make room for them. Neither of them paid any attention to the papers and folders that went flying off the desk, landing in a mess on the floor that the two of them would dread having to reorganize later.

Tracey wrapped her legs around Rob's waist, running her fingers through his silky blond hair as he fumbled with the buttons on his pants.

"We shouldn't be doing this," Tracey murmured after pulling away from the kiss for a brief moment, though her words were useless as she leaned forward again, opening her mouth to allow his tongue to slip inside.

The building was nearly empty anyway, and Tracey's office was up on the top floor. If they were quick enough, they'd be able to finish without being interrupted by yet another helpless employee coming in to ask yet another question that they should already know the answer to.

"We can stop if you want to," Rob offered anyway upon breaking their kiss to pull Tracey's top over her head. Her locs fell over her shoulders as Rob flung the shirt to the side, and he gently pushed them behind her back before unhooking her bra with one hand.

Tracey didn't answer, instead focusing on pulling Rob's cock through the hole in his unbuttoned pants. She sucked in a quiet breath as it sprang out, already glistening wet with precum, the tip of it an angry red color.

Rob had been waiting desperately for the moment that he'd finally get to have her for months now, and no matter how many times he'd jerked off to the thought of her, he'd never been able to fully satisfy his needs. He felt as if he would lose his mind if he didn't get to have her soon, and Tracey felt the exact same way.

Her panties were soaked through, Rob discovered as soon as he'd pushed his hand up her skirt, cupping the mound of flesh between her legs. She spread her thighs farther apart, moaning into his mouth as he pushed her panties to the side and gave her clit a small pinch.

Her hips rolled on their own accord as she tried to grind against his hand, desperate for more friction, more relief, more pleasure. But Rob pulled his hand away before she could find a steady rhythm, and

Tracey let out a quiet whine as she was suddenly left with nothing.

"Fuck," Rob practically whispered after pushing two fingers into his mouth. "You taste so good." His eyes darkened as he stared into Tracey's, and Tracey's mouth fell open as he brought the hand down to wrap around his cock, stroking it a few times to get it nice and wet.

He hooked his arms underneath her thighs afterward, dragging her closer to the edge of the desk and lining himself up with her entrance quickly.

"Are you ready?" he asked in between planting kisses on her lips.

"Yes, yes, yes." She nodded quickly. "I want you inside me now!"

"Shit," Rob groaned as he rubbed the head of his cock up and down her center a few times before finally pressing it inside her eager hole. Tracey's breath hitched as Rob slowly sank inside of her, inch by inch, stretching her open around the large width of his cock.

"Oh my—Fuck," she cursed before Rob's lips were pressed over hers again, his tongue darting into her mouth as he pulled her even closer.

Rob didn't waste any time before starting up a steady pace, his hips slamming into her behind with every thrust. Tracey kept her arms wrapped tightly around his neck to keep herself from flying off the desk from the force of his thrusts. The desk creaked and screeched under their weight with every movement, and Tracey's picture frames and pen holders fell to the floor when Rob pushed her to lie on her back instead, but neither of them paid it any mind, too caught up in how good it felt to finally be with each other in this capacity.

"So big," Tracey practically purred when the two of them pulled away from their kiss, letting out a short giggle which turned into a moan the moment Rob's hand trailed up her stomach to cup her breast. "Fuck, you're—so big. Stretching me out so m-much!"

Rob let out a grunt, his hips stuttering for just a moment as Tracey clenched around him. "Tight," he gritted out. "You're tight—and wet. Can feel you dripping all over my cock. What's got you so excited, hm? What, do you like being fucked over your desk like this? I bet you do. I bet you fucking love it."

"Fuck," Tracey whined, throwing her head back as she began rolling her hips in time to meet Rob's thrusts. "Mm—Yeah, I love it! I love it, I love you fucking me o-on my desk!" She hiccuped, gasping as Rob wrapped a hand around her neck.

His grip wasn't tight enough to restrict her breathing, but it was firm enough to make all the tension practically evaporate from her body as she easily submitted to him.

Rob groaned, letting out a quiet stream of curses as he looked down at where their bodies connected and watched his cock disappear and reappear inside of her pretty cunt over and over again. His balls banged against her ass with every thrust, the sound of skin slapping against skin filling the room as he slammed into her repeatedly, and the sound was only covered by Tracey's loud moans, which Rob muffled with his mouth as he leaned down to kiss her again.

Her lips were addictive, and he couldn't resist the urge to slot his lips between hers, claiming her mouth with his own every chance he got.

Tracey tried her best to kiss him back, but she could hardly do more than hold her mouth open for him to explore as he continued pounding into her quickly, the head of his cock hitting just the right spot inside her to make her eyes roll back, her body beginning to quiver as she struggled to take a full breath. She let out a screech, her whole body jolting when Rob pulled away and licked his fingers before rubbing her clit, and she squeezed her legs tightly around his waist, her back arching as her orgasm rapidly approached.

She was so close. Right there. Just about to reach her climax when everything came to a stop. Rob suddenly stopped moving, his eyes widening as he quickly pressed a hand over Tracey's mouth. Tracey didn't understand why at first, but then she heard it.

A knock, and a muffled voice on the other side of the door calling out, "Tracey? Are you busy? Can I come in? I just have a quick question about some of the paperwork you sent me this morning..."

Tracey wasn't sure whether to laugh or cry. Just like that, her orgasm had been ruined and ripped away from her just before she managed to have it.

"Whoever that is, they're fired!" she whisper-yelled.

The annoyed look on her face was priceless, and Rob would have laughed if not for the fact that the door was unlocked and the two of them were still...connected.

"Answer them!" Rob whispered back, and Tracey huffed before clearing her throat and trying to make herself sound normal.

"I'm super busy right now! Just come back by tomorrow morning, and I'll talk to you about it then!"

"All right...Are you okay? I heard some noise—"

"I'm rearranging my office!" she shouted, her eyes widening as she looked at Rob and shrugged her shoulders.

"Okay...Have a good day then," the employee called. Silence spread throughout the room as Tracey and Rob stared at each other, chests heaving from all the exertion and from the anxiety of almost being caught.

It was at least two minutes later before either of them bothered to move a muscle, and Tracey was the first one to snap out of it, slapping Rob's chest until he got the message and moved away from her.

When she stood up, Rob began tucking his cock back into his pants, assuming that she was no longer interested in having sex in the middle of her office where anyone could catch them. But instead, Tracey ran over to her door, opened it to poke her head outside and make sure there was no one around, then closed and locked it before running back to her desk and bending over it.

"Come on," she grumbled unceremoniously. "Hurry up, I want to cum now!"

"Wow, so sexy," Rob teased.

His breath caught in his throat a moment later when she reached back to spread her cheeks apart, looking back at him as she showed off her glistening pussy. Rob growled as he stepped toward her, giving his cock a couple of strokes before lining it up with her entrance again.

Tracey held her breath and put a hand over her mouth to keep herself quiet this time, and Rob chuckled as he slid back inside of her easily.

"It's useless, you know. You'll be screaming again in just a minute."

"Oh, be quiet. Don't get too cocky because I'll have you know—" Tracey's words were cut off by the sound of her own moaning. Rob pressed a hand against her lower back to keep her down as he began fucking her quickly, pulling her hips back as he pushed his own forward, and he kicked her legs farther apart with his foot to give himself better access too.

The wind was knocked out of Tracey with the force of Rob's thrusts, and the sharp edge of the desk was digging into her stomach as he held her down with a tight grip and refused to let her squirm away for even a second, but the uncomfortable feeling was hardly noticeable as Tracey focused on the feeling of Rob's cock ramming into her G-spot over and over again.

"What was that?" Rob called breathlessly, smirking as he leaned over Tracey, resting most of his weight on her back. Tracey squeezed her eyes shut, her mouth falling open as Rob's cock was pushed even deeper inside of her with the sudden change of position. "Don't get too cocky because you'll have me know…What?"

Tracey couldn't have answered him even if she'd wanted to. She was too busy drooling and mumbling incoherently as she tried to form some sort of sentence without being able to think of any words. Her mind was completely blank as her body moved on its own accord. Her legs trembled as she stood on her tippy toes, her cunt spasming around Rob's cock as her skin burned, sweat dripping down it and mixing with his.

"Rob," she moaned in between slurred words that Rob couldn't quite make out. "Cumming, cumming—Fuck, oh my God!" she stammered before slapping a hand over her mouth again.

Rob cursed under his breath, running a hand down her back and massaging her sides as he fucked her through it. The way her body slumped, exhausted after the way her climax had been punched out of her only turned Rob on even more. She was completely pliant beneath him, loud moans turning into soft whimpers as he continued rocking into her.

"Off, off," she murmured tiredly after a few minutes, pushing at his stomach. Rob quickly slid out of her, backing away until she had enough room to stand up. She turned around to face him and dropped to her knees, immediately wrapping a hand around the base of his cock and giving him a few tugs before sticking out her tongue.

"Ah—fuck," Rob groaned, clutching the edge of the desk to keep himself steady as she pumped him quickly, staring up at him with deep brown eyes and an open mouth, ready to catch all his seed.

Rob let out another low groan before cumming with a shudder that wracked through his whole body. His cock twitched, bobbing for a moment before his cum came shooting out, and Tracey moaned as she caught every bit of it that she could with her tongue.

Rob held on to her head, watching as some of his cum dripped off her tongue and onto her chest before she closed her mouth to swallow quickly. The rest of his cum landed over her lips, and when he was finished, her tongue darted out to lick up the mess.

The moment she stood up again, Rob pulled her in for another kiss, his tongue licking into her mouth and sliding over hers. He groaned as he tasted himself in their kiss, his softening cock twitching weakly as he thought about returning the favor and eating her out.

When he pushed a hand under her thigh, trying to lift her up onto the desk again, she quickly stopped him, pulling away with a tired giggle.

"We'd better not," she murmured before pausing for a moment. "I mean, not here! One close call is already one too many for me."

"Right...You're right," Rob muttered even as he wrapped his arms around her waist, sliding his hands down her back and groping her behind.

She rested her forehead against his chest, biting her lip as his wandering fingers dipped between her cheeks, gently rubbing over her cunt before moving away again.

"So—so your place?" she squeaked.

He let out a deep chuckle that Tracey tried to pretend didn't make her want to fuck him all over again before raising a brow at her. "You want to come back to my place?"

"Well, you've been begging me to for months now," she shot back. "I guess I might as well now that I finally can...And are you really sure about that? Are you sure it's a good idea to quit your job just to—"

"We've already been over this." He shrugged. "I don't care about this job nearly as much as I care about you. I'm sure I'll be able to find something elsewhere. You can write me a letter of recommendation. After the way I fucked you, I'm sure you'd like to be able to sing my praises anyway."

Tracey rolled her eyes, pushing him away from her before turning to try and find her shirt among the mess on the floor. She sighed as she noticed just how much of a mess they'd managed to make. She'd forgotten all about the coffee mug that'd been sitting on her desk, and now there would likely be a stain on her floor for the rest of her time here in the office. The email that she'd been drafting before he came was now just a mess of random keyboard smashes. And the room quite obviously smelled of sex.

"I shouldn't write a damn thing for you," she grumbled under her breath. "We're gonna have to stay late just to clean this up! The one day I was supposed to be going home early..."

"You weren't complaining when I had you bent over the—Okay, I'm sorry," Rob quickly held his hands up when Tracey shot him a cold look. "I could make it up to you if you want." He wiggled his brows.

Tracey smirked. "And how are you going to do that?"

# Sorry, Daddy
## By Lisa Wilton James

"Perfect, perfect, perfect," Katie murmured to herself as she ran her fingers through her red hair and fixed the tiniest smear of red lipstick on the corner of her lips. "Everything has to be perfect. Okay...Okay." She closed her eyes and let out a deep breath, shaking her head as she realized that she was being ridiculous.

She had a habit of talking to herself when she was nervous, along with running around like a madwoman and always needing to fumble with something in order to keep herself busy.

"This is fine," she muttered as she smoothed down her miniskirt and readjusted the bra-like top that she'd changed into after deciding that the previous ten shirts weren't good enough. "At least I look hot. It'll be fine."

She did look perfect.

She'd spent an almost embarrassing amount of time in the bathroom doing her skincare and pampering herself almost to the extent to which she did before going to a photoshoot or walking a runway. She'd done her makeup to perfection, with heavy liner and a dramatic eyeshadow, and with drawn-on freckles to take the place of the natural ones that her foundation had covered. She'd styled her hair just the way her man liked it–with pretty beach waves that looked effortless and flowed down her back beautifully. She'd put together a slutty outfit that she knew her boyfriend would like too. A simple, black bralette and a matching mini skirt with gold waist chains and high heels to match. William loved when she wore mini skirts and high heels together.

This was going to be fine.

"Oh my God!" she whisper-yelled, suddenly panicking when she heard William's car pulling into the garage. His least favorite car, to be exact. The one that he hardly ever drove because, really, he'd gifted it to Katie once she'd officially become his girlfriend since he never used it anyway, but Katie had begged to drive his car today instead, simply because she'd never driven it before and had always thought that it was cool.

And now...she was majorly regretting it. She wished that he'd just told her no again like he usually did. She wished she'd never opened her big mouth—*Oh, what are you so worried about? I'll take perfect care of it! It'll come back in better condition than it left in!*—Fuck. He was going to be so pissed off when she told him that she'd wrecked his precious sports car!

"Maybe it's not too late to flee," Katie murmured to herself as she eyed the front door. "I can just–"

She could hear William's keys rattling as he unlocked the door, and she had barely a second to react before it was pushed open and William was walking in, letting out a sigh. He looked tired from a long day, and once he'd hung his coat up and locked eyes with Katie, he immediately narrowed them.

"Katie, why do you look even hotter than usual?" he questioned suspiciously. "And does it have anything to do with the fact that my car isn't in the garage?"

"You're so silly." Katie let out an unnatural-sounding laugh as she scurried over to him, standing on her tippy toes to give him a kiss. "You look so handsome! How was work today? Let me grab your slippers for you!"

She slipped out of his eyesight and hustled her way over to the shoe cabinet, grabbing his slippers before practically sprinting back over to him to help him get them on.

"Work was tiring. I have a roster full of incompetent employees, which makes my job much more difficult. Why are you being weird?"

"I'm not being weird." Katie let out another robotic laugh before grabbing his hand and practically dragging him through the living room and into the kitchen. "I'm sorry you didn't have a great day, but you're in luck! I cooked your favorite meal for you, Daddy!" she practically purred, sending him a flirtatious wink before pushing him to sit down in his chair.

"Daddy?" He raised his brow. He was now even more suspicious than he had been just a second before. It wasn't like he wasn't used to Katie calling him Daddy; it was just that she usually reserved the word for the bedroom, or for when she was in the mood to get him in the mood, or for when she was teasing him about the fact that he was so much older than her, or for when she was in major trouble and wanted to butter him up before telling him whatever bad news she had to tell him. He had a feeling that it was the latter tonight. "Katie–"

"Shh, no talking." She grinned as she took a seat on his lap. Somehow, she'd managed to produce a cigar from what seemed like thin air. She clipped it, pressed it between his lips, and lit it before he could even react, then leaned toward the table to grab a shot glass and pour him a drink. "Whiskey?"

William let out a defeated sigh. Katie was nothing if not determined, and William had already had a stressful day as it was. Maybe it wouldn't be so bad to allow himself to be pampered for a little while before dealing with...whatever it was that he was going to have to deal with.

He took a puff of his cigar and nodded his head. "Yes, please."

Katie grinned, happily pouring him a shot of whiskey–and then three more once he'd finished the first. She played with the hair at the nape of his neck before allowing her fingers to travel into his thick head of hair, massaging the scalp. She pressed gentle kisses all over his face, then his neck, then his lips. She massaged his shoulders and squirmed around on his lap, pretending that she didn't realize that it was exciting him. And when she finally pulled her hands away from him, it was only to cut into his steak before it could start to get cold.

"Rare, just like you like it!" She smiled as she fed him a piece. "And I put six kinds of cheese into the mac and cheese, and I put shrimp, crab meat, and lobster meat on your loaded potato, just like you love it–Oh, and you're never going to guess what I made for dessert!"

William hummed lazily as he chewed the next bite of his steak. "What is it?"

"Red velvet cake with–"

"No." He let out a quiet chuckle. "I meant what is it? What did you do? You might as well tell me now and get it over with."

"I worked hard to cook this meal," Katie pouted, 'accidentally' grinding against William's obvious erection. "You could at least enjoy it first before asking so many questions."

William went back to chewing, deciding to humor Katie even as his curiosity piqued. He allowed himself to be handfed throughout dinner and dessert until his stomach was so full that he felt as if he might pop. The food was amazing, as much as he hated to admit it, and his eyes were beginning to droop by the time he'd finished.

Katie smiled. "Oh, you look so tired! Here, why

don't I just go run you a nice bath, and then I can give you a massage with all your favorite massage oils, and then you can go to bed feeling all relaxed and wake up tomorrow feeling well-rested and–"

"What did you do?" William repeated his previous question, tugging Katie to sit down again once she tried to stand up. He held her in place with an arm wrapped around her waist, eyes glaring into hers as he tried to read her. "Obviously, it's something to do with my car," he sighed. "Sweetheart, just be honest. If you scratched it, it's fine. It's been due for a paint job anyway."

Katie hummed thoughtfully as her eyebrows shot up in surprise. Maybe her attempt at buttering him up had worked better than she'd thought. Any other time, he would have thought of a scratch on his precious car as a life-or-death situation. Clearly, the rare steak and red velvet cake had managed to tame him a bit.

Unfortunately, it probably hadn't been enough to keep him calm while she told him about what had actually happened.

"Well, Daddy...It was a bit more than just a small scratch." She sent him a tearful look, her best set of puppy dog eyes and pouty lips.

"How...much more than just a small scratch?" His brow twitched.

"Well...Okay, so it's a really funny story, but I was at the mall earlier today, and I was just about to pull out of my parking spot when this absolute maniac came flying past, and I was terrified that they were going to hit me, so I quickly pressed the gas to go forward again and–and I kind of...Rammed into the pole that I'd been parked in front of...And now the entire front of your car is, ugh...Well, you can hardly even tell that it's a car anymore, I'm just going to be honest." She giggled nervously.

William's expression was unreadable. Katie couldn't tell whether he was pissed off, seconds away from bursting into tears, or if he'd even heard what she'd said at all. For the most part, his face was blank.

She squirmed around, this time without the intention of getting him hard. She was just uncomfortable as a heavy silence spread throughout the room and he continued staring her down with a billion different emotions swirling around in his eyes.

That car was like his baby. He'd had it for years now, and it'd been one of the first lavish gifts that he'd ever purchased for himself after becoming the

CEO of a major company. Plus, it had always been his dream car.

"I'm so sorry!" Katie cried, real tears beginning to slide down her cheeks. "Really, I am! I didn't mean to–I didn't know that I was going to–I never would have asked to drive it if I'd known that I was going to do something so stupid and–What can I do to earn your forgiveness, Daddy? I'll do anything! I'm so, so sorry, and I promise, I'll do anything to make this up to you! I know it won't be the same, but I can buy you a new one? I-I can crash my own car too? So, like–you know, like an eye for an eye type of thing? I can–"

"Ah," William hissed as she bounced in his lap, her ass brushing over his still-prominent erection yet again.

"Sorry, sorry, I'll move," she sniffled, and William's mouth formed an O shape as he thought of something.

"I know how you can make it up to me," he murmured after a while. "Well, it'll be a start, at least."

"Okay!" She nodded quickly. "Whatever you want! I'll do anything!"

He smirked. "Yeah, you will."

\* \* \*

Don't get him wrong, he was still pissed off and majorly devastated about what had happened to his car, but this almost made it all worth it.

He'd been begging Katie for car sex for ages now, and she'd always said no because she didn't want to ruin her precious seats. But as she had said earlier, this was an eye for an eye.

"Slow down," he groaned, his voice strained as he threw his head back against the seat. "I want to enjoy it for as long as I can."

Katie narrowed her eyes at him. She wanted to argue that he'd already been enjoying himself for quite a long time. She'd given him a lengthy blowjob earlier when they'd first come out to the car, and it had resulted in him cumming all over her face, chest, and expensive leather seats. Now she was riding him in the passenger seat and had been for the last forty-five minutes. She'd already had two orgasms, and now she was exhausted, but William knew just as well as she did that she wasn't going to stop until she'd managed to make him cum too. Which is why he'd been holding out for so long.

Nevertheless, she slowed down her movements and pushed herself all the way down on his cock, rolling her hips back and forth slowly enough for her body's trembling to be noticeable. William eyed her with a lazy smile, watching as she shuddered and jolted while she continued grinding against him.

She always looked so beautiful on top, with her perky breasts bouncing together with every one of her movements, her toned stomach flexing as she tensed up, and her face stuck in a pleasured expression as she experimented, trying to figure out what felt best for both her and him. By now, she'd learned just how to ride him in order to make him cum quickly, but he'd purposely been preventing her from doing that. He enjoyed messing with her instead.

Pushing his hips up to thrust into her randomly resulted in her letting out a yelp and leaning forward to grip his shoulders as she tried to catch her breath. Reaching down to pinch her clit between his thumb and forefinger when she was least expecting it caused her to go still, her whole body locking up as her eyes rolled back. He watched closely for any sign that she was about to have her orgasm and then grabbed her hips to hold her still, effectively ruining it before it could even have a chance of fully forming.

And every time he did, he had the pleasure of hearing her cry out for him, a desperate, whimpered,"Daddy!" that went straight to his cock.

"You're so sensitive now, aren't you?" he cooed as he pushed his hand between the two of them, rubbing at her wet cunt and chuckling when she flinched and let out a whiny moan. "You're never going to be able to make me cum like this, pathetic little thing." He sent her a sympathetic look before patting her sides. "All right, up. Get in the backseat for me."

Sure, the backseat was covered in his cum, but she didn't hesitate to climb off his lap and lie down right in the center of the mess. She lay on her stomach, ass slowly wiggling in the air as she eyed him.

"Come on, Daddy," she grumbled impatiently. "Want you to fuck me now!"

He would usually tease her for being so blunt, but she looked so beautiful sprawled out on the backseat for him with her miniskirt bunched up around her waist and her high heels pressed against the window that he didn't even bother.

He pushed himself out of his seat and climbed to the back, straddling her legs and stroking his cock as he eyed her glistening, pink pussy. "Fuck," he groaned as he pushed his way inside of her again, watching as her hole stretched around his cock, taking him in easily.

Katie moaned as William leaned down, pressing

his front to her back, caging her body between his own and the sticky car seat. William reached around, hooking two of his fingers inside her mouth and pressing down on her tongue as he began moving, fucking into her with rapid thrusts, groaning in her ear as she drooled around his fingers.

"Daddy!" Katie moaned, clutching at his arm. "Shit–I'm so close, I'm so close!" she said, already shivering beneath him. Her senses were overwhelmed with the humidity that had filled the air in the car, the smell of sex, the sound of the seats squeaking as he pressed her farther into them, his deep voice filling her ears, and the sticky wetness that seemed to be everywhere. The cum still drying on her face and now on her stomach, the drool pooling around his fingers as they remained in her mouth, her own wetness between her legs making things infinitely more slippery...

Katie felt filthy and used, and she couldn't for the life of her understand why she hadn't agreed to do this much sooner, but she'd have to figure that out later because for right now, she was more interested in fucking herself back on William's cock and chasing after her impending orgasm.

"So fucking tight," William grunted, smacking her ass just to hear her squeak. "But you won't be when I'm finished with you. I'm going to fuck you until your hole is loose and abused and not tight enough to keep my big dick inside. You've got a long way to go before I forgive you for wrecking my car, sweetheart."

That didn't sound like such a bad thing to Katie. She could get used to him fucking her like this even more often.

"Wish I could cum inside you," he whispered in her ear. "You deserve to be nothing more than my sweet little cum dump." But he pulled out of her anyway, suddenly backing away from her, which caused her to whine. He was no longer on top of her, and she could already feel her orgasm dissipating as his cock slid out of her, no longer pressed up against her G-spot.

She looked back at him, wearing a sharp glare as she watched him stroke himself quickly with one hand while kneading her ass with the other. It didn't take long before he spilled all over her ass cheeks, his cum splattering over the soft flesh and rolling down between her legs soon after.

While he was panting and groaning and cursing as his body twitched and trembled, Katie was lying as still as a board, pent-up frustration making her feel as if she was overheating. The only stimulation she got was a stray drop of cum that landed on her clit, causing her hole to clench for a moment, but aside from that...she had nothing.

And she wasn't even surprised when William wore a satisfied smirk after he'd finished cumming, making no attempt to touch her again as he unlocked the car door.

"Should we head in and have a shower?" he asked.

"I hate you!" she cried. "Are we even now?"

# Afterword

Hey friends! It's Rayna again.

I really hope you enjoyed this new collection. If you did, I'd really appreciate a review. It only takes a minute, and it really helps people find my work. Leaving a review is a giant help!

And don't forget to check out my other anthologies. Just search "Rayna Russell" on Amazon or Audible.

And lastly, I welcome all your feedback. Drop me an email at RaynaRussellErotica@gmail.com

And if you want to submit a story, I'd love to read it! 3000 words is the sweet spot.

Thanks again for taking this ride with me. I hope you enjoyed the hell out of it!

XOXO,
   Rayna

Made in United States
North Haven, CT
29 September 2023